Sudden fear had ̶̶̶̶̶̶̶̶̶̶ **erotic play of their lips together. "Aristide?"**

"What *pedhaki mou?*"

"This isn't just a one-night stand, is it? You won't disappear once we've made love?" She didn't know what made her ask the question, maybe her ongoing fear that this man was so far out of her league he belonged on another planet.

He stopped moving and held her still to meet his gaze, his expression so serious that she shivered. "I am making you mine."

LUCY MONROE started reading at age four. After going through the children's books at home, her mother caught her reading adult novels pilfered from the higher shelves on the bookcase… alas, it was nine years before she got her hands on a Harlequin romance her older sister had brought home. She loves to create the strong alpha males and independent women that people Harlequin books. When she's not immersed in a romance novel—whether reading or writing it—she enjoys travel with her family, having tea with the neighbors, gardening and visits from her numerous nieces and nephews.

Lucy loves to hear from readers.
E-mail: LucyMonroe@LucyMonroe.com
Web: www.LucyMonroe.com

Lucy Monroe

THE GREEK'S CHRISTMAS BABY

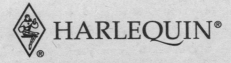

TORONTO • NEW YORK • LONDON
AMSTERDAM • PARIS • SYDNEY • HAMBURG
STOCKHOLM • ATHENS • TOKYO • MILAN • MADRID
PRAGUE • WARSAW • BUDAPEST • AUCKLAND

For Carolyn Wahl, a treasured friend and
very special woman. I couldn't think of a more
appropriate person to dedicate a Christmas book
to than one who loves Christmas as much or more
than I do. Blessings to you, dear friend!

ISBN 0-373-12506-2

THE GREEK'S CHRISTMAS BABY

First North American Publication 2005.

This edition published by arrangement with Harlequin Books S.A.

® and TM are trademarks of the publisher. Trademarks indicated with
® are registered in the United States Patent and Trademark Office, the
Canadian Trade Marks Office and in other countries.

www.eHarlequin.com

Printed in U.S.A.

CHAPTER ONE

"She's coming out of it."

Eden heard the words, but didn't recognize the voice. Her eyelids felt glued together over a layer of sandpaper. It took a Herculean effort to force them apart and, at first, all she saw was white light and moving shadows.

There were more words, but they sounded like they were coming from under water.

Someone moved to her right. "Yes, Doctor."

Her eyes began to adjust, making recognizable interpretations of the light and shadows.

A young doctor bent over her, his pale blue eyes intent on her face. "Hello, Mrs Kouros. I'm Adam Lewis, the doctor on call when you were brought in. How do you feel?"

"Like I've been hit by a truck," she rasped. Her tongue felt parched and swollen.

"You were…or at least your car was."

Images flashed in her mind. Driving rain, a wet road, the sound of squealing tires. Headlights coming straight at them. The grating honk of a car's horn, long and penetrating. Aristide swearing in Greek and English. His arm coming out to shield her, the airbags rendering the gesture superfluous. Her brown hair swirling around her face, it and the airbag blocking everything else from view.

More distressing images bombarded her and her hand moved restlessly to cover her still-flat stomach.

Her gray eyes clung to the doctor's, begging reassurance. "My baby?"

The paramedics had said the tiny life inside her probably wouldn't survive the trauma, but she'd prayed desperately they were wrong. She didn't remember anything from that desperate prayer until waking up just now.

"You're still pregnant."

"Thank God," she said brokenly, relief pouring through her slight body.

"Unfortunately, you're spotting. The good news is that there is no amniotic fluid in the blood. However, the amniotic sac has disengaged from the wall of your womb in one place. We'll do everything we can to save the baby, but the next seventy-two hours are going to be critical. You must remain in this bed and stay calm."

She nodded and winced at the ache in her head. "Hurts…"

"Yes." He shone a small flashlight in her eyes and made a note on her chart. "You're suffering a minor concussion and have several small abrasions on your right arm from shattered glass."

Now that he mentioned it, her arm did sting, but her entire body felt like she'd been beaten.

Where was Aristide? Surely he wouldn't leave her to face this alone. He might not love her, but he adored being a father. Even after their argument, he would be by her bedside for the baby's sake.

"Where is my husband?"

The doctor laid his hand on her forearm. "You must remain calm, are we agreed on that?"

"Yes." She willed her emotions in check, despite fear trying to take a choke-hold on her. "Please tell me."

"Mr Kouros is in a room down the hall. His vitals aren't bad, but he hasn't come round yet."

"He's in a coma?"

"Yes."

She flinched as if the word had been a physical blow. She felt like it had been. Prior to the accident she'd convinced herself and told Aristide that she was ready for her marriage to end. She had believed there was no greater pain than loving a man she was certain cared for another woman, but she had been wrong.

The prospect of Aristide dying hurt much worse.

"Will he come out of it?" She could barely make herself ask the question, she was so terrified of the answer.

"There's no way to tell, but indications are good."

"I need to see him." If she could see him, it would be all right. It had to be all right.

"Not just yet. As I said before, moving you would be detrimental to your pregnancy. You must remain here."

"How can I stay here while Aristide is in a coma in another room?" She struggled to sit up.

He pressed gently against her shoulders, putting a halt to her feeble efforts. "Your husband will continue to live without you by his side, but, if you attempt to go to him, your baby might not. When he wakes up, we will bring him to you."

She appreciated the "when" rather than the doctor saying "if", but his promise was not enough. "Please…isn't there some way you can take me to him?"

"Your baby's life depends on you remaining calm and remaining flat on your back in this bed," the doctor said too firmly for her to ignore.

She gave up trying to move. "Seventy-two hours?"

"If he hasn't woken up by then and you are no longer spotting, we will arrange for you to be taken to his room to sit beside his bed."

She knew she had to be strong, but it was so hard. She just wanted everything to be the way it had been before she got married, when she thought Aristide was just poor at expressing his emotions toward her...before she'd decided he didn't have any.

The doctor squeezed her shoulder in comfort before stepping back. "Bed rest is the best chance you have of ensuring the viability of your pregnancy at this point, Mrs Kouros. I know it is difficult, *but you must stay here*. We will keep you apprised of your husband's progress. I promise."

"Thank you." She blinked away tears at the kind understanding she saw reflected in the doctor's eyes. "I need to make a phone call."

"Of course."

She called her mother-in-law. Phillippa was frantic at the news of the accident and Aristide's coma. Even so, she did not neglect to ask how Eden was doing.

"I'm fine. Some minor complications...a concussion... it will keep me on bed rest for a few days, though." The only family member who knew she was pregnant was Aristide and she had every intention of keeping it that way.

She'd found out very recently herself and the news had come as a total shock. She was still breast-feeding Theo, or had been, but her milk had stopped producing and she'd gone to her doctor to find out why. She'd been dumbfounded to discover she was pregnant again so soon after the birth of her first child. Theo was only nine months old.

Even if it had been a planned event, she would have hesitated to impart news of her pregnancy to her mother-in-law when there was a chance it would end in grief.

Her heart contracted at the thought and she sent yet another desperate prayer heavenward.

"I'm so glad Theo is staying with you."

"You must not worry about your son. All is well."

Eden actually managed a smile; thoughts of her son always gave her pleasure. "Thank you."

It had been murder leaving him behind and she went to sleep every night with images of his baby features, so like his father's, firmly fixed in her mind's eye. Theo shared Aristide's dark curly hair and olive complexion, but he had her gray eyes. She missed him like crazy, but she had intended this trip to New York to be an opportunity to cement her relationship with Aristide.

She had thought that by coming back to where they had met and been lovers, she could recapture the way things had been between them. However, the trip had been a dismal failure. She'd ended up playing second fiddle to Kassandra…again, and getting so mad about it, she'd asked Aristide for a divorce.

She could barely believe she'd done it. She'd been crazy in love with him from practically the moment they met. She'd thought he felt the same way. He'd certainly acted like it.

They'd bumped into each other in front of the Metropolitan Museum of Art. It had been a muggy day in summer and Eden was visiting her dad in the city. He was busy in a last-minute business meeting and had cancelled their plans for lunch. There was nothing new in that and she'd taken herself off to the museum as she'd done on so many occasions in the past.

Only this time, she'd never made it inside.

* * *

Busy thinking, Eden let her instincts guide her toward her destination. Now that Dad had cancelled lunch, she'd have time to meet with that new glass artist she'd heard about. Would he be open to showing his work in the upcoming "History of Glass in Art" exhibit at the small museum she worked for in upstate New York? Not all artists were open to museum exhibition.

There was little to no money in it for them, but the exposure was good.

She was composing her approach to the artist in her mind when she hit what felt like a brick wall and bounced backward. Her gaze flew up as two strong, masculine hands grasped her shoulders and prevented her from falling.

Not a brick wall. A man. The most stunningly gorgeous male specimen she had ever seen. Easily six foot four, the dark-haired Adonis had eyes the color of blue lapis and a finely sculpted body encased in an Armani suit of perfect fit. He even smelled gorgeous. *Wow.* She thought maybe she mouthed the word, but wasn't sure.

He smiled down at her and she felt all the air go whooshing from her lungs while the blood rushed from her head. Dizzy, she could only be grateful he had kept his hold on her shoulders.

Those incredible blue eyes skated over her features with tactile intensity. "Excuse me, I did not intend to nearly knock you over."

But she knew, *just knew*, it had been the other way around.

"I wasn't watching where I was walking," she admitted with a grimace while she fought a totally inappropriate urge to reach out and touch the hard body so close to her own.

"And I was too busy watching you to notice the direction my steps took me." He spoke with a slight accent she could not place, his words infinitely more formal than the average American businessman.

She stared. "Did you really just say that?"

His smile grew to such sexy proportions, she was in danger of melting in a puddle at his feet. "You are unused to the men around you being honest in their attraction to you?"

"I'm not used to men like you being attracted to me at all." As soon as she blurted the words, she blushed so hotly she felt like her cheeks were on fire. She couldn't have been more gauche if she'd tried.

He didn't seem to notice. In fact, he was shaking his head, his eyes speaking messages she had to be misinterpreting. "You are teasing me, no?"

"No. I'm not very good at that sort of thing."

This made him laugh. "You are charmingly honest."

"Whereas you are embarrassingly so," she muttered, not at all sure how to take this man's attitude.

He opened his mouth to speak, but his cell phone rang. He frowned. "Excuse me for a moment."

She went to move away, but he kept one hand firmly on her shoulder while flipping his phone open with the other. She had no trouble reading his expression then. He was silently telling her to stay right where she was and arrogantly assumed she'd do it as he turned his attention to his phone call.

Her heartbeat tripled at his continued nearness and the knowledge she didn't want to go anywhere.

He started speaking in another language, one she could not place any more successfully than she had placed the accent.

He didn't talk very long before hanging up the phone and then smiling at her once again. "I must apologize. It was my assistant."

"If you need to go…"

He shook his head. "No. I find my afternoon free. My hope is to spend it with you."

Totally unprepared for that claim, she shook her head, trying to clear it.

"You have another engagement?"

"No. I…" She swallowed. "A guy like you…you don't have free afternoons."

"A guy like me, *pethi mou*?"

"What does that mean?" she asked, diverted.

"*Pethi mou?* Loosely translated, it means my little one."

"In what language?"

"I am Greek."

"Oh," she sighed out. She should have realized. He was every bit as yummy as any statuary she'd ever seen of the Greek gods. More so, if she was honest with herself.

"Now, answer me…what do you mean by *a guy like me*?"

"A businessman…a corporate shark."

"You think I am a shark?"

She looked at his clothes, took in the familiar aura surrounding him, and then remembered the way he'd wielded his cell phone and how effectively he'd controlled her with a mere look. "Yeah."

"And do you have a lot of experience with guys like me?" Incredibly, he sounded jealous.

She almost laughed, but didn't think he'd appreciate the humor of the situation. "Not a lot, no. But my dad is one and I used to work for him."

"No longer?"

"No. I work for a museum in upstate New York now."

"So, you are not from the city?"

She shook her head. "I'm supposed to be visiting my dad, but something came up." And then, incredibly, she found herself telling him her other errand and he offered to go with her to see the artist.

It was mad, but she wanted desperately to say yes, to prolong this meeting between total strangers.

He read her hesitation and asked, "Your father is into big business?"

"Yes."

The gorgeous Greek handed her his phone. "Call him. Tell him that Aristide Kouros wants you to spend the afternoon with him."

His absolute assurance her father would know who he was and vouch for him surprised her, but maybe it shouldn't have. This guy was not lacking in confidence in any way.

"That's your name? Aristide?" she asked to put off making the call, trying to decide if she wanted to.

This man was dangerous, but so delectable she wasn't sure that was going to matter to her.

"Yes."

"My name is Eden."

Aristide's hand moved to cup her nape and his thumb brushed along her jaw. "That is a lovely name."

Her breathing fractured and she stuttered out, "Th-thank y-you."

He pressed the phone into her hand. "Call."

She did. Her father did indeed know who Aristide was and asked to speak to him. She couldn't tell much from Aristide's side of the conversation, but when she got the phone back, her father told her the other man was trustworthy.

"But he's out of your league, honey. Be careful."

"It's not safe to go with him?" she asked.

Aristide frowned, his body stiffening with offense, and she could just tell he wanted to grab the phone back from her and tell her dad a thing or two.

"I didn't say that," her dad was saying. "He's safe to your person, but your heart is another matter. He makes me seem like a tame pussycat."

That did give her pause. Her dad hadn't gotten serious with anyone since her mom, though he'd had numerous affairs, and the truth was, he hadn't been faithful to her mom, either. Was Aristide the philandering type?

One look into his burning blue gaze and she had to doubt that assessment.

Nevertheless, she was biting her lip when Aristide took the phone from her and flipped it shut.

She sighed. "He says I'm not in your league."

"You are in your own league, Eden. You are special."

"You don't know me, how can you say that?"

"Are you saying your reaction to me is like any you have had to another man?"

"No."

"Special."

"Yes."

"Do you think I make a routine practice of clearing my heavy schedule to spend time getting to know a woman I bump into on the street?"

Put like that… It should be impossible for something like this to happen so fast, but it *was* happening. "I guess I can accept that this is unique for you."

"*You* are unique for me."

And she had believed him, Eden thought as she lay in her hospital bed, memories washing over her. From that point on, he'd certainly treated her like she was special. They spent the day together and he didn't press to take her to bed that night. Honesty made her admit to herself that, if he had, she would have been a total pushover.

But he hadn't and she had stayed over in New York City for the weekend, which they spent together.

Then she had to go home.

She didn't know if she would see him again, but she had. He'd called several times that week and then surprised her by coming to see her in upstate New York. He'd wined and dined her, his every casual touch sending her libido to places it had never been. They talked for hours, discovering they liked the same foods, enjoyed the same movies and he was fascinated by her knowledge and interest in antiques.

When he took her home that night, he'd started making love to her and she'd gone under with all the buoyancy of a rock tossed into a stormy sea.

Remembering that first time made her heart palpitate even now.

Eden had waited in silence while Aristide unlocked the door to her apartment. The sexual tension in the air was so thick, it pressed against her like a physical force. He wanted her, but she wanted him too. More than she'd ever wanted another man…enough even to silence her clamoring nerves and internal worries that all of this was moving way too fast.

The look of dark promise in his deep blue eyes said he didn't think it was moving fast enough. "I like your place."

She looked around. Her home was the middle floor of a tri-story Victorian-era house that had been converted into three separate apartments. Carved wooden trim painted white and walls painted in deep rich tones gave her home an elegance that she had fallen in love with on first viewing the property.

She'd broken up the high gloss of the hardwood floors with antique oriental throw rugs in tones complementary to the walls. All of her furniture had an oriental motif, but it didn't feel modern. She'd scoured flea markets and antique stores all over the state to decorate with inlaid lacquer pieces and furnishings that gave the impression of the ancient culture of the Far East.

"I'm glad you like it. I do too."

He'd shut the door and locked it and now turned to face her, his hands divesting her of her jacket while his eyes devoured her. "I like you even more."

She licked her suddenly dry lips. "I like you too."

"I'm going to kiss you, *pethi mou*."

"All right."

But when his lips touched hers, it was unlike anything she'd ever known. Even with him. This kiss was claimstaking at its most basic. His hands curled around her waist and pulled her body into his while his tongue demanded entry into her mouth. She gave it to him.

From the first slide of his tongue against hers the passion he sparked in her burned through her body to singe every single, solitary nerve ending into sizzling life and she went up in flames. It was too much, but not enough, and she whimpered as she undulated against him in wanton abandon.

He groaned and one hand moved down to cup her bottom, massaging her and causing a burst of heated humidity between her legs. Their clothes fell away as if by magic and then she was standing naked in the circle of his arms.

Sudden fear had her breaking the erotic play of their lips together. "Aristide?"

"What, *pedhaki mou*?"

"This isn't just a one-night stand, is it? You won't disappear once we've made love?" She didn't know what made her ask the question, maybe her ongoing fear that this man was so far out of her league he belonged on another planet.

He stopped moving and held her still to meet his gaze, his expression so serious that she shivered. "I am making you mine, not preparing to notch a bloody bedpost."

She bit her lip. "Do you become mine too?"

"Of course."

She shuddered. "Okay."

It wasn't a promise of forever, but it was also not the age-old "no ties" out-clause of the commitment-shy male. He wanted more than a temporary slaking of physical need. She was glad because her feelings for him demanded it be more while at the same time making it nearly impossible to say no, regardless of what his intentions were.

They came together in a conflagration of need that broke through her virginal barrier with her barely even realizing it had occurred. The pain was minimal and incredible pleasure followed it almost immediately. Their lovemaking culminated in a completion so intense, she was insensate afterward.

She slowly became aware of him again as he kissed her all over her face and throat, saying over and over again that she was beautiful, passionate and *his*. The claiming lasted throughout the long night of her sexual awakening.

The next morning, he woke her with a kiss that was so tender it made her cry. He laughed when she explained her tears were because his lovemaking was so beautiful, his masculine arrogance basking in her overt approval.

And, as promised, their time together was in no way related to a one-night stand. He'd told her she was special and proved it. He had an even more demanding schedule than her dad, but he called her at least once a day. He spent almost every weekend with her, sometimes bringing her to New York City, but usually he came to her apartment despite it being a two-hour drive.

He treated her like a queen and made love to her like she was the most irresistible woman on the planet.

He willingly got to know her father. While they had actually met briefly in the business arena, they now became friends. She and Aristide were together months before she started to wonder about him introducing her to his family. The couple of times she had brought it up, he put it off, saying he wanted to keep her to himself and she believed him.

His life was so hectic, so high pressure that she got a charge out of being what he called "his oasis" in the desert of a life filled with the grains of sand that comprised his business and family commitments.

However, as the months grew to a year and he made trips back to Greece without ever once inviting her, she started to wonder about her role in his life. How necessary was an "oasis" and did him seeing her that way mean she was a mirage that would disappear from his life at some point in the future?

Unlike when he was living in New York, he rarely called her from Greece and never made any overt commitment to return to her when he left. But she knew if he did, she would be waiting. She loved him and her life, at least, was not complete without him. He left a huge void when he was gone and she felt like she walked around as half of a person until they were together again.

It gave her a frightening sense of vulnerability, one she was certain he did not share.

She discovered she was pregnant during one of the trips he took to Greece without her. She knew right away she was keeping the baby, but she was worried about telling Aristide. He'd been so careful about contraception and she couldn't help wondering if he would balk at her taking a more permanent role in his life…that of his child's mother.

She told him of the pregnancy his first day back. He'd come to see her straight from the airport and she took that as a good sign. They made love and were lying entwined in her bed when she told him about the baby.

She was curled into his side, sated and so filled with love for him, she was bursting with it. "I've got something I need to tell you."

He moved so he was leaning over her and met her gaze with his own, his eyes compelling her to honesty. "This sounds serious. What is it?"

"I'm pregnant."

He went completely still, the vibrant blue of his irises disappearing almost completely as his pupils dilated in shock. "But…"

"Contraceptives fail," was all she could think to say.

Then he was smiling brilliantly, the change in his demeanor happening so fast, she was stunned. "You are carrying my child? Why did you not call and tell me?"

"It's not something you say over the phone." Not to mention the fact she had never once felt comfortable calling him at his office in Greece or on his cell phone when he was abroad.

He nodded, his expression filled with blatant pleasure now. "I understand. This is amazing."

"I'm glad you feel that way."

"How else could I feel?"

"Trapped?" she suggested.

But he just laughed. "We'll get married as soon as possible."

As marriage proposals went, it lacked romance, but she was so relieved he wanted to spend the rest of his life with her, she didn't quibble. She loved him so much; regardless of the doubts that had plagued her over the last few months, he had to love her too.

He'd been too instantaneous in the marriage decision and for a guy like him to stay with one girlfriend so long had to be significant.

"All right. I'll marry you."

CHAPTER TWO

EDEN MOVED restlessly in her hospital bed as she remembered her naïve assumptions. Aristide had moved her to Greece right after the wedding, introducing her to his family, a wonderful group of people who had accepted her without a qualm.

But the fairytale marriage situation ended there, because she saw less of her husband than she had of her lover. He spent as much time in New York as before, but now she was an ocean away. He called her frequently, but that did not assuage the lonely ache in her heart left by his absence.

At first, she had not traveled with him because of her morning sickness, but then he had told her he didn't want her uncomfortable, making the long flight in an advanced state of pregnancy. After the birth of their son, she had opted to breast-feed, which meant she went nowhere without Theo, and Aristide did not believe a tiny baby should make the long flight to the States.

In addition to the separations her new role in his life dictated, Kassandra had entered her life.

Kassandra and Aristide had grown up together and then the beautiful Greek woman had started working for his company. She'd been his personal assistant for the last five years. While Eden and Aristide were only lovers, Kassandra ignored Eden's existence, but that ended almost immediately after her marriage. Not that Eden had latched on to the change right away.

But looking back, she could see that Kassandra had begun enacting subtle ploys to undermine Eden's confidence and Aristide's time spent with her from the very first.

When Eden first began to suspect the other woman of manipulation, she had convinced herself she was imagining the other woman's malice. Everyone liked Kassandra. The family. The other people who worked with Aristide.

And Kassandra was so sweet to Eden on the surface that it had taken almost a full year before she realized the Greek woman really had it in for her marriage. Even then, she hadn't known what to do about it. She had not wanted to rock the boat in her relationship with Aristide, but the more convinced she became that her husband had married her simply for the sake of their son, the less quiescent she felt about Kassandra's machinations.

It had all come to a head in New York and Eden had complained for the first time about Kassandra. Bitterly and without pulling any punches. She now realized she'd been a fool to bottle it up for so long and not say anything. Her grievances had fallen on deaf ears because Aristide had thought she was out of her mind.

He trusted his assistant. Why shouldn't he? He'd known her for a lot longer than he'd known his wife and she'd never before shown this devious side to her personality.

But Eden had lost her ability to put up with Kassandra's manipulations when the other woman arranged to usurp Eden at Aristide's side for a Broadway performance they had planned to attend. Kassandra had turned the evening into a business event and Aristide had expected Eden to gracefully back out of attending the play with him.

She had been livid and refused and they had had the worst fight of their marriage. She had accused him of being in love with the other woman. He had told Eden she was being both childish and selfish and flat-out refused to reconsider taking Kassandra to the play. Eden had rejected his peace offering of changing the entire seating arrangements to include one more person and had stayed in the hotel rather than go with them.

The following morning, they were driving upstate to spend the weekend away from his business pressures when Eden again voiced her grievances. Aristide had dismissed her complaints as if they were ludicrous. He had not taken her seriously at all and the more he stonewalled her, the angrier she became, until the rage inside her gave vent to a demand for a divorce.

In her desperation to be heard, she had believed they were the only words that might penetrate his stubborn Greek skull. She'd been right. He'd listened all right. He'd been shouting at her in rapid-fire Greek she couldn't begin to decipher when they were hit by the truck.

Eden now recognized how poorly she had handled the confrontation with her husband. She should have built up to it, pointing out Kassandra's undermining as they went along instead of hitting Aristide with it all at once in what he considered a fantastic claim. But if she'd messed up, so had he.

He had rejected her claims outright and had not taken her seriously at all…not until she said she wanted a divorce. He'd been paying attention then, and remembering his look of horror gave her a small measure of hope.

Aristide did not want their marriage to end. But she did

not know if that was because he was a typically possessive Greek male who wanted to raise his children in a two-parent household, or if he personally could not stand the thought of losing Eden. It was a question she could no longer stand to go unanswered.

She was pregnant again, just like before, but this time she wasn't going to bury her head in the sand, making assumptions about his feelings based on his actions. She wanted the words. She had to know…one way or the other.

As scared as she was of both losing her baby and of Aristide's coma, she was also filled with determination. She was going to rock the boat on her marriage until her husband got seasick and sent the wicked witch flying off on her broomstick…or until he admitted he would rather have Kassandra in his life than Eden.

The accident had clarified a lot of things in her head. She wasn't giving up on her marriage, but she wasn't playing the doormat wife any more. She wasn't going through another pregnancy like the last one, where she got left behind in Greece "for her own good" while he worked in New York more than half the time.

Nor would she tolerate Kassandra's constant belittling of her, no matter how subtly the woman played it. She didn't think Aristide was sleeping with his assistant, but the other woman had too much of his loyalty. There was fidelity of mind as well as body and Eden was determined to have both from her husband.

Aristide was a wonderful father and there was nothing she wanted more than for him to be with her to raise their children, but he lacked in the husband department and it was time that changed.

She had lacked as a wife too, she saw now. She'd been too afraid to incur his anger to stand up for herself, too unsure of her place in his life to demand it fully. She wasn't going to be that way any more. She deserved better and so did he.

Marriage had changed her, she saw now. She'd wanted so desperately to gain Aristide's love and make it work that she'd become a woman she didn't always recognize or like any more. The change had begun during her time as Aristide's lover, but she didn't care what had made it start, she wanted it stopped.

She wasn't going to end up like her mother. *She wasn't.*

The next three days went by in a haze for Eden. Aristide did not wake up and every hour he laid in a coma in another hospital room, her heart bled a little more. She loved him so much and the thought of even trying to live without him sent her blood pressure skyrocketing, incurring a long lecture from the doctor.

His family had arrived and taken up residence in the hotel, but spent most of their time at the hospital. Phillippa had brought Theo and, thankfully, Rachel willingly cared for him with her own two children while at the hotel. She brought Theo in to visit Eden and that helped, but she could not forget for one second that her husband's life remained precarious.

She ached with the need to be by his bedside, but did her best to remain still and calm to retain the unstable hold she had on her baby.

Her father called from Hong Kong, where he was away on business. Once he learned her injuries were not life threatening, he made it clear he had no intention of flying home early on her account. She was hardly surprised by his lack of overt concern. As with Aristide, she had always taken a poor second to business with her father.

The doctor kept his promise and apprised Eden each morning and evening of Aristide's condition, no matter that she had frequent updates from his family. He was kind and she found his visits less stressful than Aristide's family. She did not have to hide her condition or worry for her baby from him and Adam Lewis turned out to be an unexpected friend.

Leaning heavily on Sebastian's arm for balance, Eden made her way slowly down the hall toward her husband's room. She'd refused to use a wheelchair, not wanting him to think the worst when he saw her and possibly suffer a setback because of it.

Adam had told her that Aristide had not asked about the baby, but that didn't mean he wasn't thinking about it. It was just like her strong husband to hide his worries, even from a doctor.

But her bleeding had stopped completely and the latest ultrasound had come back with good news. The doctor had assured her the short walk would not hurt the baby, but, due to her lingering concussion, she still wasn't supposed to be up and walking around a great deal.

Nevertheless, she'd taken a shower and washed her hair, leaving it to fall in a straight brown curtain around her shoulders. Aristide preferred that style and she was so happy he had woken from the coma, she wanted to please him. She had donned a set of pajamas that could pass for loungewear. She hoped Aristide wouldn't notice the IV shunt in her hand before she had a chance to tell him all was well with the baby.

No one had told him that she was in hospital as well and, according to his mother, he hadn't asked. Eden found that very odd, but then maybe he was still angry at her for bringing up divorce. She could see his pride balking at her temerity and she almost smiled.

They had a lot to discuss, but right now all she wanted to do was see the man she'd married and assure herself he truly was awake and going to be all right.

She walked into the room, her eyes hungry for the sight of the man she loved. She'd missed him so much during the hours of loneliness in her hospital bed while memories, both good and painful, filled her mind, reminding her just how much she would be giving up if she let her husband go.

Nothing could assuage the perpetual ache in Eden's heart left by her husband's absence. Which said a lot about the probability of her ever walking away from her marriage if there was *any* chance at making it work.

Aristide was sitting up in bed and tears of relief wet her eyes. She'd tried so hard to remain emotionally detached from his coma, but she'd been scared to death she would save her baby only to lose her husband.

His dark head was visible because of his height, but Kassandra Helios stood at the head of the bed, blocking Eden's view of his face.

She had always felt at a disadvantage next to the other woman and even more so now. Eden's looks were average, no matter what Aristide said in the midst of passion. But right now she knew her pale complexion could best be described as wan and her nondescript gray eyes were dull from her concussion.

The last thing she wanted right now was to face her nemesis. "I thought only family were allowed to visit critical-care patients."

The moment the words left her mouth, she regretted them. Too many people in this room considered Kassandra exactly that.

Kassandra turned, her smile imbued with so much false sympathy Eden had a sudden urge to be sick that could not be blamed entirely on morning sickness. "Surely I qualify. I've known him longer than any other woman in his life besides his mother…why, we're practically brother and sister."

Eden couldn't argue the claim, but she didn't buy it. The sly witch felt sisterly toward Aristide in a pig's eye. However, she bit back the retort she wanted to make. Now was not the time to take her stand against the enemy.

Before she had a chance to reply in any way, Kassandra spoke again. "We are friends as well and I have been so worried," she said with an affecting break in her voice. "I have barely stirred from his side. It did not occur to me to make myself scarce now…that I would be unwelcome."

"Eden did not mean to imply any such thing," Phillippa said. "I'm sure she spoke merely out of surprise."

"We all know you have been a good friend to Aristide as well as an employee," Sebastian added in a soothing voice.

Eden felt like a monster, even though she knew it was all nothing more than a cleverly portrayed act. Kassandra's place within the Kouros clan was unassailable. No one saw her manipulations for what they were, but Eden was heartily tired of being wrong-footed by the Greek paragon.

Stubbornly determined not to apologize when she was not in the wrong, Eden inclined her head to Kassandra. The Greek woman made no effort to move, so Eden stepped around her in order to see Aristide properly. But she pulled up short at the total lack of recognition in her husband's brilliant blue eyes.

"Who are you and where do you get off censuring Kassandra for being here?"

The angry words whirled around in her head and she felt as if she'd taken a body blow. "W-what?"

He turned his irate gaze to his brother. "Who the hell is this, Sebastian? She's not Rachel and that's the only woman that should be hanging on to your arm like it's a lifeline."

Even sitting in the hospital bed having just woken from a coma, Aristide's powerful vitality emanated in waves from his tall, muscular body. His genuine lack of recognition was just as palpable a force.

"You don't know who I am?" she asked faintly.

"No. Should I?" he demanded. "I do not appreciate you coming into my room and upsetting my visitors."

Someone gasped. She thought it might have been Phillippa, but she couldn't turn her head to find out. She was paralyzed with shock and reeling inside from a pain she'd never expected to feel. She swayed on her feet, her vision blurring as her skin grew clammy with shock.

"He doesn't remember me," she said to no one in particular, the words coming out in a whisper as her body sagged against her brother-in-law.

Strong hands stopped her fall, but that was the last thing she remembered until she woke in her bed some minutes later.

Phillippa was standing over her, worry etched in her beautiful Greek features. "Eden?"

"Why didn't you tell me he has amnesia?" she asked painfully. "I could have—" She bit off the words before revealing her pregnancy.

"We didn't know he did. He talked about Theo just as he always does…he knew all of us."

"So, it's only me he doesn't remember? That makes no sense. How can he remember his son and not the woman who gave birth to him?"

Adam put down her wrist after checking her pulse. "Apparently, it wasn't something he thought about until his family explained who you are."

That didn't ring true. Aristide wouldn't let that kind of inconsistency in his memory stand, but then he'd only woken from his coma forty-five minutes before she'd entered his room.

"He's confused."

"Yes."

"I'm sure he'll remember me now."

The doctor shook his head and Phillippa's eyes filled with tears. "He refused to believe us when we told him that you are his wife."

Eden couldn't breathe. She moaned, her head thrashing from side to side. "No…he *has* to remember me."

"Confusion and a temporary loss of memory are not uncommon side effects with a head injury like he sustained in the accident." Adam gripped her hand with both urgency and reassurance, his kindness warming her. "And it's still not a good idea to allow *yourself* to become upset."

"My husband refuses to believe I am his wife and you expect me to stay calm?" she demanded, shaken to her soul by the implications of Aristide's memory loss.

"I'm sorry," the doctor said before insisting on giving her a pregnancy-safe sedative so she would sleep.

She woke the next morning, remembering the horror of being the only person her husband had forgotten.

When the doctor came in for rounds, he told her that Aristide's head injury didn't explain the selective amnesia. "It doesn't fit with any of the usual patterns for post-head-trauma amnesia."

"I see. Have you been able to convince him of who I am?"

"Your brother-in-law took that job on before I had a chance to tell him not to." The doctor looked less than pleased by that state of affairs.

"Why would you want to wait?"

"We don't know what's causing the lack of memory, but any emotional upheaval is risky for an amnesia patient."

"And did learning he has a wife he doesn't remember upset him?" she couldn't help asking.

"Not that we could tell." Adam sighed, as if realizing the news would be unwelcome to her. "Apparently, now that he's had time to think about it, the knowledge makes the existence of his son more sensible to him."

That sounded like Aristide.

"Does he want to see me?"

"He's trying to come to terms with his memory loss."

"What does that mean?" She couldn't take it in. "Are you saying he *doesn't* want to see me?" That was completely out of character for her husband.

He always wanted every piece of information concerning any situation. For him not to want to see her felt like the most directed of rejections, no matter what he could or could not remember.

"Not at present, no."

Pain coalesced inside her at the confirmation until there was a knot of it where her heart should be. "And Kassandra?"

"Do you mean Miss Helios?"

"Yes."

"She's a frequent visitor. I understand she is an old family friend who works for him."

The monitor beside the bed started beeping and Adam's pale gaze sharpened with concern. "You need to remain calm. The news is disconcerting, I know…but, given enough time, he will remember you. It may even be sooner than later. *You* are not out of the woods yet, though. You still have a concussion and your baby is doing well, but an emotional trauma on top of the physical one could be devastating to your pregnancy."

"I'm sure you are right." But she didn't know how to stop herself from being upset.

If she'd ever needed proof positive that Aristide didn't love her and had stayed in their marriage for their son's sake, she had it now. He remembered everyone but the wife he obviously wished he could forget.

Correction...*had* forgotten.

Three days later, Eden couldn't stand waiting any longer and decided to visit her husband in his hospital room even though he'd made no indication he wanted to see her.

She'd checked out of the hospital the day before with a clean bill of health and been told that normal activity should not put her baby at risk. The doctor had even made the joke that a little stress wouldn't hurt the baby, so it was safe to go home and be a full-time mom to her nine-month-old again.

She hadn't been able to laugh. Her relief at her own restored health was heavily tempered by Aristide's continued memory loss.

She'd dressed with care for this meeting. Eden's slight curves did not lend themselves to the kind of sexy apparel that looked good on so many other women, but she had done her best with what she had.

She wasn't showing her pregnancy yet and, if it followed the path of the one she'd had with Theo, there would be very little outward evidence until her fifth month. So, she'd opted to don a figure-hugging dress in gray-blue cashmere with long sleeves and a skirt that stopped well above her knee. Aristide had said it was one of his favorites and she didn't get to wear it often in Greece. It was too warm.

Her shoes were basic black pumps, but their three-inch heels made her legs look longer. Five feet five might be average for a woman's height, but Eden often felt like a shrimp around the much taller Aristide.

She pushed his private room's door open without knocking and was greeted by a tableau to make any wife's heart catch in her chest. Kassandra sat on the bed, coaxing Aristide to eat his lunch.

Eden could not believe the pain she felt at the cozy scene. Aristide had not asked to see her, effectively banning her from his room by his silence, while Kassandra was not only welcome, but welcome to behave toward him with an intimacy that should have been reserved for his wife.

It should have been her sitting on that bed, but Aristide hadn't wanted her and the knowledge hurt beyond bearing. Once again, she had been relegated to a secondary role in his life and knowing he didn't remember her only exacerbated the pain, not lessened it.

Even worse, he had forgotten the child she carried, as if the reminder of how inexorably their lives were linked was something he could not bear. She felt as if someone had taken a shredder to her emotions and she had no idea how to find any sort of happiness again.

They both looked up at her entrance, neither registering the slightest guilt, and anger washed over her. "I didn't realize your assistant's duties ran to playing nursemaid."

Aristide's blue eyes darkened with displeasure. "Why not? You certainly were not here to do it."

How dare he throw her absence from his hospital room back on her? If it had been up to her, she would have been here non-stop from the moment the doctor had said it was all right. *"You didn't ask for me."*

"And that stopped you from coming to the side of your husband's hospital bed?" he derided. "You are here now and still I have not asked for you."

Kassandra got up and walked toward Eden. "I think this is my cue to leave. I don't want to be the cause of another domestic disturbance."

She implied there'd been many, when in fact Eden had tolerated far too much in the name of harmony. She gritted her teeth to stop from saying so. Adam had made it clear that she was not to upset his patient, going so far as to instruct her unequivocally not to tell Aristide about the baby.

Bad enough Aristide had forgotten their child, but she must refrain from reminding him of the baby's existence. It was just another poisoned dart of pain that had found its way with the unerring accuracy of a bull's-eye to her heart. As kind as Adam had been to her, his concern for her husband was just as acute.

Kassandra's smug expression worried Eden and she couldn't help wondering what the poisonous witch had been telling Aristide. Eden waited until the other woman was less than a foot away before stepping aside to let her leave the room.

She turned and spoke in a low voice that would not carry to her husband's ears. "You get what you give, Kassandra."

The other woman's eyes widened, as if she couldn't believe Eden had dared to say anything in front of Aristide, then she smiled maliciously. "Oh, I will get what's coming to me all right. Just as soon as you let go of him."

It was the first time Kassandra had stated her intentions so blatantly, but they didn't surprise Eden, not by a long shot.

"That's not going to happen. I'm never letting him go. Not ever."

Kassandra smiled, her expression mocking. "I think you will. Besides, who said you would get a choice in the matter?"

Without another word, Eden spun on her heel and headed toward the bed and a husband that did not remember her, but whom she loved with every fiber of her being.

She wasn't letting Kassandra have him without a fight, but she couldn't help feeling she shouldn't have to fight for a man who had promised her a lifetime of fidelity. She'd kept her end of their marriage bargain, giving him a son and her heart.

She only hoped he had kept his. Ever since she'd come to the conclusion that he married her for the sake of their child, she had wondered if his feelings had never engaged for her because they were held elsewhere. Only, if he loved Kassandra, why had he made Eden his lover?

Was it a Greek thing? It was hard to believe, but maybe Kassandra was still a virgin. Aristide would not take her to bed without marrying her in that case. The thought she'd been nothing more than a sexual diversion gone wrong made bile rise in her sensitive stomach.

She stopped when her legs brushed the side of his bed. "The doctor said you would be released tomorrow."

He stared at her through eyes that had always had the power to mesmerize her, his expression impassive. "Yes." He shoved the tray of hospital food away. "I will finish the meetings here that the accident interrupted and then return to Greece."

Not *we*, but *I*. Looking for a distraction from the disturbing syntax, she focused on his hardly eaten lunch.

"Is that all you plan to eat?"

"Yes."

"Surely you shouldn't be skipping meals. You need to regain your strength."

"I am fine. And if you are so concerned about my health, perhaps you should not have been so quick to frighten off the woman convincing me to eat this tasteless mess."

Her frighten Kassandra? Not in this lifetime.

"Are you telling me you need someone to entice you to eat?" Eden mocked.

"Maybe I do. Are you prepared to take on the job?" His tone said he didn't see how *she* could cajole him into anything.

She'd been married to him for sixteen months and raising his son, who was very much like him, for nine of those months. He might not remember her, but she wasn't so handicapped. A woman who cared could learn an awful lot about her husband in that amount of time, and Eden cared…a lot.

She slipped her coat off and laid it over the chair beside the bed before taking the place Kassandra had vacated. Gritting her teeth at the scent of the other woman lingering around her, Eden reached out and touched his lips in a move he would have recognized as quite daring for her.

If he'd been able to remember.

"I know how to feed all of your hungers, darling." Her voice was husky with a promise she hoped he would remember on an instinctual level.

His eyes turned a familiar midnight-blue and his jaw

went taut like it did when he was trying to hold back desire.

She wasn't unaffected either. Even this small touch sent electric jolts of remembered intimacy throughout her body. It had always been like this—their reaction to one another had been cataclysmic and instantaneous from the first moment.

Without warning, Aristide jerked his head back, his eyes narrowing, the contempt in them unmistakable. "Is this how you trapped me into marriage? Using your body?"

CHAPTER THREE

THE SHOCK those words caused reverberated through her.

She let her hand drop. "I wasn't the one doing the seducing in our relationship."

"Kassandra implied you trapped me into marriage with the oldest trick in the book. Is that true?" he asked, sounding disgusted. "Did I marry you because you were pregnant with my child?"

So, Kassandra *had* been busy spreading tales. Eden wasn't surprised, but it hurt to think Aristide had listened with both ears open to the other woman's vitriol.

Eden gritted her teeth, wishing she could deny his accusation, but she couldn't. Not now that she herself had come to accept the truth. "Yes. You married me because I was pregnant with Theo. *But it was no trap.* I did not get pregnant on purpose."

Aristide frowned fiercely at her, his disbelief obvious. His attitude was far removed from that of the lover she had known for nearly three years. He had never once doubted her word before, not even when she told him she was pregnant with his baby. He could have accused her of seeing someone else while he was gone on his frequent and often extended business travels, but he hadn't.

He hadn't even implied it was a possibility.

He'd always treated her with respect, like she mattered. Maybe not as much as Kouros Industries, but more than an afterthought he couldn't be bothered to see while he was in hospital.

Had his patience toward her and proclaimed acceptance of her role in his life all been an act?

It was hard to believe anything else now.

"You love your son," she couldn't help saying, as if somehow that affection should reflect on her as well.

She knew it didn't. Hadn't she always known? But still there was a part of her that persisted in hoping. How stupid was that?

Aristide's expression hardened. "I am aware of it. *I remember him.*"

Well, that was telling her. Sharpened talons of pain clawed through her, piercing the barely inflated balloon of hope. "Yes, of course."

Her quiet acknowledgement seemed to make him uncomfortable and he shifted restlessly in the bed. "If nothing else, I owe you gratitude for giving me such a wonderful child."

His thanks was the last thing she could bear. She needed his love and now she didn't even have his memory. She stood up, unable to withstand any more. It had been a mistake to come here. One more in a long line of them, starting with her agreement to marry a man who had never once told her he loved her.

"You owe me nothing. I love our son every bit as much as you do." She grabbed her coat and started putting it back on.

But he seized her arm, stopping her from finishing the task. "Where do you think you are going?"

"Back to the hotel. It's obvious my company is surplus to requirements." She hated the weakness the catch in her voice revealed to him.

She had to get out of there.

"Like hell. You are my wife and this is the first time you have deigned to visit me in three days. You are not walking out after a perfunctory five minutes."

"You didn't want me to come." She could not stop hot tears from filling her eyes, but she tried to blink them back. "Y-you told the doctor."

"And that upset you?" he asked with a supreme lack of tact.

"Of course it did." How could he be so cruel? Even if he didn't remember her, was he totally insensitive to what a woman in her position would be going through right now? *"I love you.* How could this *not* upset me?"

"You love me?" he asked with derision she did not deserve. "The evidence is not in your favor. You were nowhere around when I was in a coma. No one told you to stay away then."

"I was in my own hospital bed."

"With minor complications. A concussion, I believe. If you loved me, would you not have had your bed and mine in the same room so you could be here, hoping for my awakening?"

She'd never once considered her absence from his bedside might affect him this way. Evidently, he'd taken it as proof positive she wasn't the wife she should be. And right at that moment, she could not make herself care. What difference did it make? He obviously had never wanted to be married to her in the first place.

But even as angry as she was, part of her wanted to exonerate herself by telling him of her pregnancy and the ordered bed rest. However, Adam had been very explicit…no revelations of that sort until Aristide regained his memory or they understood better why he'd lost it.

And she had to wonder if it would make a difference. He clearly had expected her to get a bed in his room for treating her concussion—would the reason for her bed rest make any difference to him? Probably not.

"It didn't occur to me," she admitted with pained honesty, just wanting to leave.

"Perhaps it should have."

"Apparently, but we aren't all brilliant tycoons with a penchant for solving logistics problems even while under sedation for our injuries."

"I do not appreciate your sarcasm."

"I'm sure you don't, but then you don't seem to appreciate anything at all about me now. And let's face it…you didn't exactly miss me. You forgot I even existed in your life."

"You act as if I did it on purpose."

"Didn't you?"

"Maybe I had reason."

"Is that what Kassandra said? That I'm some kind of monster wife who so tormented your existence you had to forget me?"

His silence said it all.

"And you believed her?"

"What other reason could there be for such selective amnesia? It only makes sense that I *wanted* to forget you. That you were the kind of wife a man like me would find intolerable." He didn't sound entirely convinced, but the words were damaging all the same.

"That's a pretty big assumption," she forced out between stiff lips, cold with the shock of his revelations.

"Not made without supporting evidence."

"Maybe you wanted to forget you had a wife at all," she said, voicing her own private suspicion. "Before I got pregnant with Theo, you weren't exactly keen on commitment."

"I am not so weak." And she could tell such an image of himself did not sit well.

"Maybe there's no reason for the amnesia. Maybe it's one of those inexplicable medical things that happens sometimes."

He shook his head, rejecting her no-fault excuse. "That is not likely. The doctor can find no physical reason for the selective amnesia."

"Did Adam say he thinks you wanted to forget me?"

"Adam?"

"Doctor Lewis."

"I find it odd my wife is on first-name terms with my doctor."

"You forget, he was my doctor as well. He's been very kind to me since the accident. He knew how much your coma upset me."

"Well, even your *good friend* the doctor believes my amnesia is psychologically rather than physiologically triggered."

She let the "good friend" comment pass, not willing to be sidetracked from the point by something so insignificant. "But that doesn't necessarily follow that you forgot me because I was a bad wife. You're too smart to have married a woman that unsuitable. Surely you must see that."

She couldn't live with that possibility. Bad enough that he may have wanted to forget her simply because he had never really wanted to be married in the first place.

"I have to wonder if our marriage was the only way you would give me power in my son's life."

"You think I would use our child to blackmail you?"

He shrugged. "If that is the case, I am surprised I fell for it. After all, I had watched the Queen Piranha at work for years in her marriage to my uncle and, as you said, I am intelligent; however, love for a child may make a fool of the father."

Eden stumbled back and landed with a thump on the chair. *"You believe I'm like Andrea Demakis?"* she asked hoarsely, even more horrified by that than the idea he believed her capable of using Theo for her own ends.

There was no greater insult he could level at her.

She'd never known his uncle's wife. Both Matthias and Andrea had died in a car crash before Eden and Aristide met, but the stories about the woman were horrific. Aristide and the rest of his family had hated her. According to them, Andrea had been money-grubbing, irrational, unfaithful, entirely selfish and more egotistical than Narcissus.

The miracle was that such a woman could give birth to an incredible daughter like Rachel. Even more amazing was that Rachel had ended up married to Aristide's older brother, Sebastian Kouros. Having met her sister-in-law's father, Eden figured all the good genes had come from him. Vincent was a very special man, who had been capable of luring Phillippa from the isolation of her widowhood.

According to Aristide, their marriage was something like the eighth wonder of the world.

Adam walked in at that moment and frowned when he took in her tears and the look of frustrated anger on Aristide's face. "Eden, I was not aware your husband had asked for you."

She was beyond prevaricating, even with silence. "He didn't."

"My wife does not need to wait for an invitation to visit me." The glare Aristide gave the doctor should have singed his white lab coat. "Nor do I appreciate the familiarity of your address to her."

"I'm sorry it offends you. However, what concerns me the most is that this kind of upset isn't good for your condition," he said, indicating the two of them with a wave of his hand.

"My *condition* is a slight concussion and selective amnesia," Aristide said in a freezing tone he usually saved for the boardroom. "I fail to see how either could be hindered by a visit from my wife. Surely being in her company should jog my memory, not harm it."

"She is in tears."

"I noticed. If you leave, I can take care of that."

The doctor's brows rose at her husband's arrogance, but he nodded. "That might be best. This can't be an easy situation for either of you. I will come by later to discuss your release."

Eden scrambled to her feet, wiping her wet cheeks, embarrassed and still hurting so much she found it hard to breathe. "Don't leave, Adam. There's no need. I'm going."

She tried to pull her coat from Aristide's grip, but he wouldn't release his hold.

"Let go."

"I told you. I will not tolerate you leaving so quickly."

She'd had enough. He probably wanted the doctor to leave so he could berate her some more, but she wasn't sticking around for it. She let the coat go and rushed toward the door.

Aristide called her name in a voice heavy with frustration and demand. She ignored him and barreled out of his room, almost knocking Kassandra down in the process. The other woman had obviously been hanging around outside the door and eavesdropping.

Her smug expression said she liked what she'd heard too.

Considering how painful the interview had been for Eden, she saw red. Literally. A blood-red haze seemed to surround the tall Greek woman as Eden glared at her, incapable of making the movement that would separate them. Kassandra had done everything in her power to undermine Eden's marriage and now she was bent on destroying it completely.

But Eden wasn't going to let that happen. If she and Aristide failed in their bid to make a successful family, it would be because he didn't love Eden, not because Kassandra succeeded with her evil machinations. The woman was pure poison and it was not a poison Eden would allow to taint her marriage any longer. Desperate anger clawed at her insides. Whatever it took, she was going to fight for her marriage and for the man she loved.

"You ought to watch where you are going." Kassandra shoved her away, making no pretense of being polite or gentle and Eden fell against the wall.

Fear for her baby added to the cauldron of dark emotion boiling inside of her. "Don't ever do that again."

Kassandra appeared supremely unconcerned by Eden's anger. "Or what, Mrs Kouros? You'll tell Aristide? Do you really think he would care? I am his friend, *the woman he remembers*. He let me feed him, but he knocked you back," she said, confirming she'd been listening in on their conversation via the open door. "He doesn't mind my touch. *He trusts me*. Do you really think he'll care if I'm rude to you, or even believe you if you tell him so? He's already forgotten you. You're nothing to him. It won't be long before he's ready to kick you out of his life as quickly as he invited you into it."

Eden's mind seemed to screech to a halt at the viciously mocking words. She couldn't think. She could only feel and it was the blackest rage she'd ever known. No thought sparked her next action, just unadulterated fury. She slapped the other woman hard. The violence shocked her, but she didn't even begin to feel like apologizing.

Kassandra stumbled back, her expression stunned.

"You won't get away with it," Eden said when she could get her mouth to form words.

Kassandra's eyes narrowed. "You're wrong. I'm clever, much smarter than a woman who didn't even know enough to prevent an accidental pregnancy."

"You told him I got pregnant on purpose."

"He came to that conclusion on his own."

"But you led him there."

Kassandra's shrug said, *so what if she had?* "He should never have married you. You are not in his league and you never will be."

"One day he's going to remember. You know that, don't you?" Eden demanded. "Do not think for a minute he'll thank you for lying to him about what kind of wife I've been. Aristide's sense of honor is very important to him and he's going to be furious when he realizes you are directly responsible for him compromising it."

Kassandra smiled complacently, smug certainty of victory draping her like a cloak. "We were friends long before you met and we will be friends after you are gone. And believe me…you will be gone."

Eden stood very straight, letting all the disdain she felt for the other woman show. "*Friends* is the operative word.

I was his lover and now I'm his wife and I'm not going anywhere."

If there was something to salvage of her marriage, she would save it. If not, she would walk away because it was the right thing to do, not because she'd been sent packing by the selfish manipulator in front of her.

"I may not be his wife, but what makes you so sure I am not his lover?"

"As I said...*my husband* is a man of integrity. He wouldn't take a mistress."

He had promised her and she had believed him. She wasn't sure Aristide didn't *want* Kassandra, but she refused to believe he had taken the other woman as a mistress. Without another word or opportunity for Kassandra to vent more of her malice, Eden stormed away.

She barely made it around the corner before she was rushing for a restroom where she was violently ill. Having committed the first act of violence in her adult life, combined with the knowledge that Kassandra was relying on Aristide's lack of memory to make it possible for her to play her cruel, destructive games more blatantly than ever before, was too much for Eden's pregnancy-sensitized system.

Aristide might not be able to remember his wife, but he knew he did not like seeing her cry. Even though he had every reason to believe she was all he despised in a woman, knowing her tears were his fault made him feel like a heel. And that made him angry.

He told everyone he could not remember her at all and in a sense that was true, but once he accepted he had a wife, an overwhelming sense of foreboding came over him every time he thought about his marriage. It centered on

Eden, but he did not know what caused it or how to dispel it.

He knew only that something had been drastically wrong in his marriage and it was all too easy to believe his wife had been a carbon copy of the woman who had married his uncle.

Regardless, he got no enjoyment out of watching her walk away from him. It made him feel something very much like fear and he hated it. He feared nothing...particularly no woman. That way lay total destruction for the male of the species. He'd seen enough of it with his great-uncle.

Matthias Demakis had given his young wife way too much power in his life and she had repaid that gift by using and humiliating the old man. Both Aristide and Sebastian had learned a hard and painful lesson from Matthias's marriage to Andrea.

He glowered at the door Eden had gone through. Memory, or no memory, his wife would not bring him to his knees.

"That must have been some fight for her to go storming off without her coat. The temperature is below freezing out there and she didn't strike me as the sort of woman to storm anywhere."

Aristide's head snapped up at the sound of the doctor's voice. He didn't know how long he'd been staring at the closed door, half-expecting his wife to come back through. Though why he should, he had no idea.

"We were not fighting."

"You could have fooled me."

The tension inside Aristide increased another notch. "My relationship with my wife is not something you need to concern yourself with."

"That's not true. Your amnesia is almost certainly psychologically based, as we've discussed. I would say your relationship with Eden is key to your medical condition and your health is my responsibility."

Aristide clenched his jaw at the doctor's use of her first name again. No Greek doctor would be so familiar, but his wife and this doctor were both American. Common sense told him to leave it alone, but his male instincts shrieked for redress.

"Nevertheless," he said through gritted teeth, "I have no intention of discussing *my wife* with you."

"I cannot force you to, of course, but she's been through a lot since the accident. Your memory loss and refusal to see her has been hard on her. She's vulnerable right now. Try to remember that."

"I did not refuse to see her."

Doctor Lewis's blond brows rose. "You did."

"Once."

"You never asked for her after that."

"She is my wife. She should not require an invitation to visit my bedside."

"Perhaps someone should have told her that."

Aristide said nothing.

"Yes, well." The doctor lifted Eden's coat from where it had dropped, but Aristide still had hold of one sleeve. Doctor Lewis pulled gently. "Why don't you let me take this to her?"

Aristide forced himself to let go, an inexplicable twinge in his chest. Was the other man's interest merely that of a medical professional for a former patient, or was he attracted to Eden as a woman?

She was beautiful and if the aura of sweetness surrounding her was not genuine, she did a good job pretend-

ing. For most men, the combination would be irresistible.
The thoughts spun in his head, making it ache as the doctor strode from the room, Eden's coat clutched in one hand.

A second later, Kassandra walked back in, her cheek red. Her dark brown eyes were filled with tears and her superbly glossed lower lip trembled.

"What happened?" he asked, feeling more irritation at her reappearance than concern.

Which wasn't fair to her. She'd been a good friend his entire life and loyal employee for many years. It wasn't her fault he had this damnable selective amnesia or a wife he couldn't figure out, but was instinctively wary of.

Kassandra shook her head, her hand going to cover her cheek in a protective gesture. "Nothing."

"Tell me."

"I would rather not," she said, averting her eyes. "Things are strained enough between you and Eden as it is."

"You are saying Eden hit you?" Astonishment coursed through him. As much as he had a bad feeling whenever he thought of Eden, she had not struck him as a violent woman.

"Your wife is upset I've been spending so much time with you."

"So, she slapped you?"

Kassandra nodded with obvious reluctance. "After issuing a rather strong warning to stay away from you."

Eden's vulnerability during their discussion must have been an act along with the façade of her gentle disposition. Kassandra had certainly implied that Eden was not the sweetness and light she appeared to be. The red mark on his assistant's face would seem to indicate she saw Eden more clearly than the doctor.

Yet...part of him refused to believe despite the evidence of his eyes. It made no sense. The dark feelings surrounding Eden in his mind should make it easy for him to believe, but it wasn't. It was as if he had a mental block and that made him feel helpless. He should have no problem trusting Kassandra and her loyalty to him. He knew nothing about Eden and everything about the woman who had been in his life so long.

If only he could remember.

His head began to pound in earnest.

"Are you all right?" Kassandra asked, her hand on his arm.

Funny...her touch did nothing for him. Whereas Eden standing within a foot of his bed had impacted his libido despite all his doubts about her and the lingering effects of a concussion.

"I should be asking you that."

She smiled bravely. "I am fine. I am sure she did not mean to do any lasting damage."

"She should not have hit you. I will speak to her."

"Don't. She is already..." Kassandra paused as if looking for the right word. "Volatile, or irrational rather. It is to be expected, I am sure. Any wife would have been severely taxed emotionally by everything you have gone through."

Left unspoken was the fact that Eden had shown little of that concern in staying away from his hospital room the past week. And yet she had expressed what he would have sworn was genuine hurt over his initial request she not come back in to see him immediately. Had apparently taken that as word one on her lack of welcome at his bedside...if the doctor's interpretation was to be believed.

Aristide closed his eyes against the pain in his head. He did not know what to think and he could not trust his own judgment. Not when it came to a woman he'd forgotten so completely.

There had to be a reason for that and he could think of no other than the one Kassandra had hinted at—that Eden was the kind of wife nightmares were made of.

CHAPTER FOUR

"ARE YOU ready to go?"

Aristide turned at the sound of his wife's husky voice.

Eden had pulled her soft brown hair back in a French braid, leaving her face exposed to his view. However, her carefully controlled features and wary gray gaze told him nothing of what was in her mind, nor why she had chosen to come rather than sending his brother to see to his discharge.

She had called him last night too, ostensibly so he could tell Theo goodnight, but she had asked how Aristide was feeling and sounded genuinely interested in the answer. She had not rushed to get off the phone when he finished talking to the baby either, wanting to know what the doctor had had to say.

Aristide hadn't wanted to discuss Dr Lewis's visit, choosing instead to bring up Eden's altercation with Kassandra. When he told her how much her action displeased him, his wife's tone had gotten colder than the Arctic. She'd hung up quickly enough then after little more than a stilted goodbye.

He had not expected her to show up in his hospital room this morning.

She made no move to take her coat off, but stood ramrod straight by the door, as if ready to make a hasty exit if he made a wrong move. Either she was the best actress living, or underneath the avarice that had prompted their marriage, she was vulnerable in an unexpected way.

"I have been ready for the last hour."

She crossed her arms over her chest and tilted her chin at a defensive angle. "I'm sorry you had to wait. The doctor said ten-thirty."

Her body language screamed, *Do not touch me…stay out of my space.*

The hands-off attitude hit him on the raw, especially considering how he'd spent the morning stewing over the implied intimacy of his wife's relationship with the doctor. Aristide found himself crossing the room to pull her into his arms before he even thought about it.

He might not remember her, but this woman was his wife and no way was she going to hold back from him like he was some kind of pariah.

She gasped when their bodies collided. "What are you doing?"

She didn't sound nearly as composed as she had a moment ago and he was curiously satisfied by that reality.

His mouth hovered over hers. "Greeting my wife."

She opened her mouth and he closed his over it. He watched in fascination as her gray eyes widened and then slid shut, thick black lashes fanning her pale cheeks. He closed his eyes too, allowing sensation to take hold.

Their lips fit together with a perfection he had never known with another woman and she tasted as sweet as Christmas divinity. Not at all like a piranha wife with dollar signs in her eyes.

Her lips trembled under his and he deepened the kiss, claiming possession in a way that was wholly instinctual.

She let him, her entire body trembling now as he explored the warmth of her mouth.

He closed his hands around her waist and lifted her against him, his own body shuddering at the contact. It felt incredibly familiar when her arms locked around his neck and her tongue slid along his with tentative aggression. He couldn't believe the impact that one small touch had on him, but he was ready to toss her on the bed and make the sweetest kind of love to his forgotten wife.

Was in fact *aching* with the need to follow through on the promise of her pliant lips against his. .

He broke the kiss. "You *taste* like I know you."

"I do?" She sounded so damn hopeful, he felt his first pang of guilt for forgetting her.

"Evidently my body knows you even if my mind does not."

She winced as if the words hurt her and maybe they had. "I enjoyed it."

She let go of her hold around his neck, pressing against his chest as if she wanted him to release her. "Yes. Well, sex has never been a problem for us."

It was his turn to wince. She made it sound as if that was the only thing they got right and not like she thought that was all her fault. He had no way of denying it, but his pride smarted at the possibility.

He released her. She stepped away and, looking down, smoothed her coat. He let her get away with the small evasion, needing a moment to collect himself as well. He could not remember a simple kiss ever being so devastating to his senses. If their intimacy was always this explosive, his marriage made a lot more sense to him.

So did the birth of their son.

"I was expecting Sebastian this morning."

"He's waiting in the car."

"I did not expect you," he clarified.

"I didn't tell your family about our argument yesterday."

"So they expected you to do the honors?"

"Yes."

"Why not tell them?"

She looked at him then, her expression scornful. "You would prefer I shared our personal troubles with the others?"

She was right. He rarely revealed the most private parts of his life to anyone, even his mother and older brother. It was disconcerting to realize that while she was a complete mystery to him, she knew things about him even his closest friend wouldn't be aware of.

"No."

"I didn't think so."

"So you were doing as you thought I wanted?"

"Not really. Yesterday, I didn't particularly care what you thought."

He didn't know why, but he didn't believe her. "You did not?"

"No." She frowned at him like an evil genie and he almost expected to disappear in a puff of smoke. "I didn't buy it when the doctor said you were worried and sent him after me with my coat, either."

"He was being kind. It was his idea," Aristide said, feeling stung and conversely annoyed she was right that he had not been the one to think of her comfort.

He disliked even more the feeling of guilt that knowledge engendered in him.

She turned away, but not before he saw the look of hurt that crossed her features. "That's what I thought."

"So, why did you not tell my family if I made you so angry?"

"I didn't see any reason to increase their present turmoil." She took a deep breath and turned back to face him once more, this time her face as smooth as marble.

If her lips were not still red from his kiss, he would not be sure it had even happened.

"You Kouroses put a great store by strong marriages and family relationships. If your mother or brother thought we were having problems, it would worry them and I don't think they need any more worry right now. They've been upset enough by the accident and your loss of memory."

"Are you trying to say we should attempt a façade of the happy, loving couple in front of them?" If she knew him as well as a wife should, she would know that, though he was intensely private, he never lied to his family.

"That would be impossible, but I was hoping you would save open hostility for behind closed doors. Our son does not need to sense his mom and dad are at odds either. He's had a rough few days as well."

"Of course, but you are assuming we will continue to argue?"

"It's inevitable in the current situation."

"That does not sound like we have the most harmonious marriage."

"On the contrary. One of the reasons I'm hoping you will be reasonable about this is that neither your family, nor our son, are used to seeing us at odds. Until this trip to New York, we got along great, but my tolerance is at a very low ebb at the moment. I might even characterize it as nonexistent."

"Why is that, I wonder?"

"That isn't something I want to discuss until you've regained your memory."

"You are so sure I will challenge your tolerance?" She made it sound like he was the husband from Hades and that image of himself was not acceptable.

"As long as Kassandra Helios is in our lives, she'll do her best to instigate trouble between us. I'm no longer willing to ignore her machinations and, because of that, we're bound to fight. It's as simple as that."

"She is a long-term employee and a friend. You will not speak about her that way to me."

"Whereas I'm only your wife…that at least has not changed, memory or no memory."

Before he could answer the implied accusation in her words, the morning-shift nurse came in with a wheelchair.

"What is this for?" he demanded.

"Hospital policy," she said with a flirtatious smile that made his wife purse her lips cynically. "You have to be escorted downstairs."

Eden's eyes now glowed with provoking mockery, but she said nothing. It was obvious she knew how much he would hate the idea of being pushed in a wheelchair and found his predicament much too amusing for his liking. She obviously didn't mind his arrogance being taken down a notch, or two.

Aristide glared at her and then the nurse who had the effrontery to flirt with a married man. She'd been nauseatingly coy all morning.

"By all means, follow me with that thing and escort me, but I will not be sitting in it." He strode from the room to the sound of the nurse's anxious arguments and his wife's mocking laughter.

Eden sat in the backseat of the Mercedes and listened to Aristide and Sebastian talk business on the way to the hotel.

Aristide was every bit as savvy as he had ever been. This further evidence that he remembered everyone and everything but her added to the hurt roiling inside of her. Hurt that seemed to grow like a mushroom cloud after a nuclear explosion...out of control and with no end in sight.

Even the way he had so naturally projected the united front to his brother and the hospital staff that he had mocked in his hospital room gave her pain. He'd opened the door for her and helped her inside the car despite the fact he was the discharging patient. It had effectively made his position as her husband clear to the hospital staff and even Sebastian.

Knowing it had more to do with his pride than any real desire to align himself with her, the casual touches had nevertheless left her breathless. Her lips still tingled from his kiss as well, but she wasn't foolish enough to think that had been personal either.

She knew what that kiss had been about and it had nothing to do with undying love, or even a primal recognition that happened at a level deeper than the conscious mind. She wished she could believe it did, but she'd spent enough time in a fantasy world where her husband was concerned.

Reality was that though Aristide was a thoroughly modern man in some ways, he was as traditional as they came in others. He was also a competitive alpha male who would chase and conquer without conscious thought. He might not remember her, but he knew she was his wife. As such, he expected a certain openness from her toward him.

She'd known the mistake of her remote stance the minute that look of predatory intent came into his eyes. But she'd been angry at being taken to task over Kassandra, without ever once being asked for her own side. Eden was not a violent person. Aristide used to know that.

Telling herself he didn't remember didn't help. He never would have accused her of such a thing when they first met and were practically strangers.

So, she'd held herself aloof when she arrived in his room, only to regret her stance instantly. Only by then, it had been too late to stave off his natural instinct to establish his role as her mate. He'd kissed her and she had fallen into it like she always did, proving once again she had almost no selfprotection where he was concerned.

It was not a pleasant revelation.

Phillippa cried as she hugged Aristide. "It is so good to see you out of the hospital, my baby boy."

"Hardly a baby, Mama."

"Always…until the day I die."

Eden couldn't help smiling at the exchange…she'd seen it so many times before. "I'm sure Aristide is happy to be out of the hospital as well. We all know how much he despises confinement of any kind."

Aristide looked at her, a strange expression on his face.

Rachel grinned and hugged her big husband. "It's a Kouros male trait."

"There is one notable exception, *agape mou*." Sebastian leaned over and brushed a kiss across her brow. "Don't you think?"

"What's that?" Eden asked with a smile for the other couple, despite the prick of envy in her chest.

Sebastian looked at her while tucking his wife close into his side. "Why, marriage, of course."

Eden lost her smile and noticed Aristide had too.

"Are you all right, Eden?"

She forced a smile for her mother-in-law. "Yes. Of course."

"It is good to have him out of the hospital, is it not?"

"Yes."

Then Phillippa grimaced as if she had only now realized that for Eden having Aristide "home" was not quite the same as it was for the others.

The sound of her son talking to himself in the other room told Eden that Theo had woken from his nap. She used the excuse of fetching him to get out of the suddenly laden atmosphere.

Theo was sitting up in his portacrib. His favorite purple dinosaur in his chubby little hands, he jabbered at the stuffed animal a mile a minute in baby talk.

Taking after his father's large stature, her sturdy son was already quite a handful and Eden groaned playfully as she lifted him. "You're such a big boy."

He grabbed her shirt and tried to stand in her arms. "Mama…Mama…Mama…"

Her son's repertoire of words was by no means extensive, but what he knew he used.

Taking a firmer grip on his squirming form, she cuddled him into her body and kissed his baby-soft cheek. "How is Mommy's little man? Hmm? You are such a good baby."

She kissed him again and he hugged her around her neck.

"Mama," he sighed with obvious baby delight.

She grinned at her name on her son's lips. This was one male she never had to wonder if he loved her. Her dad's love and Aristide's might be suspect, but not this precious bundle of joy.

"Is your diaper wet, honey?" she asked as she laid him on the makeshift changing table.

He grinned and kicked his feet.

She managed to get his PJ bottoms off without incident, but then he squealed and twisted with such glee he almost fell off the changing pad. "Da...da...da...da..."

Aristide's deep laugh alerted her to his presence close behind her and a second later his big body was so near, he surrounded her with his heat.

He reached past her to brush his fingers down their son's cheek. "Hello, *agape mou.*"

Theo squealed again and twisted toward his daddy. Aristide put his hand on the baby's strong little body and held him in place, talking to Theo in Greek while Eden finished changing him. It was like so many times before that, for a second, it was as if he'd never lost his memory.

Then he stepped back and allowed her to lift the baby from the table and the sense of closeness was gone.

"Let me take him." She nodded and handed the baby over, sucking in a pain-filled breath when her husband carefully avoided touching her.

Aristide walked into the bedroom, drying his hair with a towel, and stopped dead in his tracks. "You are sleeping in here?"

Eden adjusted the blankets over her nightgown-clad form. It was a new purchase, just as the pajamas she'd worn at the hospital had been. She hadn't worn nightwear to bed since becoming his lover, but something about sleeping naked with a man who didn't remember her left her feeling too vulnerable.

"Where else would I sleep?" she asked in genuine confusion.

"Shouldn't you be sleeping in Theo's room? As you said in the hospital, our son has been through a lot of upheaval this past week."

"I've slept in the room with him the last four nights and he's been fine." Not that Theo had noticed. Their son slept like a log. "Besides, your mom and Vincent are sleeping in there now that you are here."

"Wouldn't he be more comforted if he woke in the night to find you there?"

"Theo stopped waking in the night when he was four months old."

"But these are unusual circumstances."

"Not now they aren't."

"Because I am out of the hospital?"

"Because I am and have been for the past few days. Theo is used to his daddy being gone."

Aristide frowned. "I have a job."

"That comes before everything else. I know."

"And you do not like that?"

"What woman would?" She sighed, not willing to get into something that could have no resolution in the current situation. "Look, none of that matters right now."

"It is our marriage…I do not consider that of no import."

"You don't even remember getting married."

"Which does not equate to me dismissing my responsibilities as a husband."

"Look…it's a waste of time to discuss a past you don't remember. It's not as if you're going to take my word for the way things were."

He'd made that clear enough.

He shrugged, confirming her suspicions.

Then something occurred to her that probably should have earlier, but she had not even considered it. "Do you feel awkward about sleeping with a woman who is for all intents and purposes a stranger? Of course you do. I'm such an idiot not to have thought of it before. I'll move to one of the spare rooms."

"Do not be ridiculous. You are my wife."

"But still a stranger."

He didn't say anything, but his silence was all the answer she needed.

She couldn't believe she had been dumb enough to climb into their bed as if nothing had changed between them. She'd been so wrapped up in the shock of him seeing her as a villain that she hadn't realized his questions could be masking feelings of vulnerability. Aristide would rather be boiled in oil than admit weakness.

She climbed out of bed in the heavy silence, trying not to let her hurt from this additional rejection show on her face. After all, this situation was not his fault and it was time she stopped treating him like he had done it on purpose. He may have forgotten her because subconsciously he *wanted* to, but he had no way of undoing the damage now that it was done.

He grabbed her arm before she could leave the room. "Stranger or not, you are my wife. You sleep with me."

"It's all right, Aristide. Really."

"As you said, we do not wish to upset my family. My mother will not be pleased to find you in another room in the morning."

He had a point. "I could get up before she does."

"Good luck. Even I do not."

This was true. Phillippa required less sleep than her sons, which was superhuman in Eden's mind. She looked back over her shoulder. The bed was a king-size.

They could sleep the whole night without touching. "If you're sure you won't be too uncomfortable."

"You make me sound like a nervous virgin." And that was the last way he saw himself.

She actually laughed. "I can't imagine anything further from the truth."

She turned around and gasped inaudibly as he dropped his towel and climbed into the bed.

The thought of sharing even such a big bed with his naked body and not having the right to reach out and touch him sounded more like torture than restful sleep.

She went to the opposite side of the bed from him and slid beneath the covers. She stayed as close to the edge as possible, feeling lonelier than she ever had even when Aristide was gone on a prolonged business trip.

Eventually, she fell into a fitful sleep.

Sometime in the night she migrated toward his side of the bed, waking up in the pre-dawn hours with his body wrapped around hers.

She knew she should move, would be mortified if he woke and found her on his side of the bed, but it felt so good, so safe, that she stayed. She lay there almost not breathing, not wanting to end the small bit of heaven in a series of days that could only have been dreamed up in hell itself.

She leaned forward the tiniest bit so she could inhale his scent and found herself on her back being kissed to within an inch of her life without the slightest warning.

CHAPTER FIVE

IT WASN'T the first time this had happened.

Aristide didn't even need to be fully awake to begin making love to her, but this was the first time she wasn't absolutely positive she was the woman he was making love to in his head.

She couldn't seem to make that matter, though…not with his lips devouring hers and his big, familiar body warming every square centimeter of her skin.

She dove into the kiss with all the enthusiasm of a starving woman facing a feast. Her hands roamed over his naked back and torso, touching skin that was all satin strength and heat.

Oh, man, she needed this. Affirmation that on some level, at least, they still connected.

He divested her of the nightgown she'd donned earlier and closed one sure hand over her breast. Her nipple beaded immediately against his palm, throbbing with the need for his attention. She arched her back and he took the silent hint, breaking the kiss and tasting his way down her neck to her breast. He laved the soft flesh with his tongue, teasing her until she moaned with desire. He took the hard nipple into his mouth, pressing it against the roof of his mouth with his tongue and sucking hard all at once. It felt so good, so right, that tears filled her eyes.

She dug her fingers through his silky black hair. "Oh, Aristide…my love."

He released her nipple and blew on it, making it sting with a pleasurable ache. "Baby, you taste so good," he said against her breast. Then he said something low in Greek she didn't quite catch.

But baby? He'd never called her that, not once in all the times they had made love.

Her troubled thoughts splintered as his hand delved between her thighs. Long, talented fingers pleasured her most private flesh with knowing assurance. He might not remember her, but his body remembered how she liked to be touched.

She squirmed, reaching down to touch his hardness. He was big, but she knew he fit…that he felt perfect inside her. She wrapped her fingers around him, though the tips did not quite touch.

He groaned. "That's right, baby, touch me just like that."

She gritted her teeth, but in the end couldn't stop the question. "What's my name?"

His head came up, but she couldn't read his expression, not in the dark. "What?"

"Who am I?"

"My lover."

His mouth closed over hers, the kiss all consuming, but a small part of her refused to get lost in it. No matter how good his touch and lips felt devouring hers, she needed to know it was her he was making love to and not a phantom in his mind, or worse…another woman.

After several blissful moments, he broke the kiss and

started trailing his lips down her neck toward her breasts again.

She forced herself to ask, "Who are you making love to, Aristide?"

He stopped with his lips over one aching and throbbing nipple. He lifted his head as if trying to see her expression in the dark. Maybe he could. He'd always had better night vision than she did.

"What is this about, Eden?"

Relief surged through her. "Nothing. It's all right, now." He'd called her by name. He wasn't making love in his mind to some other woman.

He was still for a heartbeat. "What was the problem?"

"You called me *baby*."

"And this is not normal?"

The fact he had to ask pierced the haze of sensual pleasure. "No. It isn't."

"What do I usually call you?"

"Eden…or *yineka mou*." How she loved that endearment that labeled her both his wife and his woman, ever since the first time he'd told her what it meant.

"I cannot call you *my woman* when I do not remember you as part of my life."

Though spoken apologetically, the words were better at dousing her ardor than a bucket of cold water. "That's true… and how can you see yourself as my husband either?"

"I don't feel like a husband." He didn't sound like that bothered him all that much, but the words tore away the last remnant of the sensual blinders she'd been wearing since waking up feeling so secure in his arms.

She pushed against him. "I can't do this."

His finger brushed over her sweetest spot, eliciting a moan. "I think you can."

"I don't want to," she said desperately.

"Why not?"

"In your heart, we aren't really married."

"But we are in my head." He grabbed her hand and touched her wedding band. "This ring proclaims you are my wife."

She pressed against the spot on his chest where his heart resided. "But this tells you that I don't belong in your life."

"I want you."

"For sex."

"What is the matter with that? You were not always so scrupulous or we would not have a son, nor would we be married. But then maybe that was planned, sex for the big payoff. Have I been paying for your *affection* since then?"

"That's a terrible thing to say." He was comparing her to Andrea in his mind again and she couldn't stand it.

"Is it? The truth is not always pretty."

Her heart was breaking, but she wouldn't cry. Not now, with him. "Get off of me."

"Why should I? I'm sure we can come to some amicable arrangement. After all, I'm a rich man and I want you. Tell me, what did you get out of me the last time we had sex?"

She hit his shoulder with her fist. "Get off!"

He rolled away and she scooted off the bed, her body shivering uncontrollably, like she was standing naked in a blizzard. But the only ice bombarding her was the shards coming straight from his heart.

"You want to know what you gave me the last time we made love?"

"Yes," he ground out cynically.

"The knowledge that I was yours and you were mine.

That you wanted *me*, not just a body. You gave me pleasure, but that pleasure wasn't about the way you touched me with your hands…though, heaven knows, you are an incredible lover. You gave me tenderness. I felt safe and appreciated, if not loved. Now, all I feel is dirty." The last words came out choked around the tears tightening her throat.

She rushed into the bathroom before he could answer.

Aristide sat up, his sexual frustration so acute, he was in pain. How dare she say he made her feel dirty?

He was her husband, not some stranger who had propositioned her. He might not remember her, but she remembered him, damn it. So, he did not feel married himself, that did not mean he wasn't. Damn illogical woman.

The sound of her sobs reached him.

Okay…so maybe he should not have goaded her that way. It wasn't as if he believed half of what he had said. No matter what kind of negative feeling hovered over him when he thought of his marriage, he knew himself well enough to know he would never stoop to paying for sex.

He felt like hell. Sexual frustration was lousy on his temper. She ought to know that, but then maybe she didn't usually tell him no. The thought made him ache.

What had he done in taunting her?

He wanted Eden, had woken up wanting her and had acted on that desire. But she had not liked him calling her *baby*. She claimed he usually called her *yineka mou*. That assertion did strange things to his insides—because, as he told her, he considered that endearment very personal.

Would he have used it on a wife he didn't want?

More importantly, why had he been so loathe to use it

now? Two words and she would have let him into her body. He was married to her, those words should not be so hard to say, but they were. Impossible, in fact.

He'd never used them with a girlfriend, not once. He was a possessive guy, but *yineka mou* implied a level of possession he had never accepted reciprocally. He had only her word he had used the phrase, but why would she lie?

Her assertion that she could not make love to him when he did not consider himself married in his heart stood his view of her on its head. Unless it was some deep strategy on her part. The whole scenario made him question the wisdom of getting involved sexually with her.

He never lied to women, not in word or action. If he made love to her, would he be implying feelings he did not have?

His sense of integrity would not allow that, nor was he comfortable with the overwhelming nature of their intimacy. He'd lost himself and been tempted to lie to her just to get inside her body. That implied she had way more power over him physically than he had ever ceded to another woman and he wasn't sure he was willing to cede it to her.

"I don't understand why Theo and I can't stay here and return with you to Greece when you are done with your business."

Aristide frowned, unwilling to voice the key reason for his request that his wife and son fly back to Greece with the rest of his family the next day.

He feared his ability to refrain from making love to her. The longer he was in her company, the more he wanted her. It was an addiction he had no intention of feeding until he understood his marriage better. Hell, he wasn't sure even then he wanted to allow her the chance to wrap him up in a prison of her subtle sensuality.

He was confused enough with the holes in his memory; he could not afford to further cloud his thought processes with sex. Even if it was mind boggling, as he suspected it would be.

Besides, his wife had made it clear she would balk at sharing her body with him when he did not remember her. She had implied she thought his amnesia was subconsciously deliberate. He'd taken that to mean she acknowledged he had reason to do so.

However, that did not mean she liked being forgotten, or would want him touching her while he couldn't remember making her a Kouros...couldn't even remember the first time they met.

"A hotel room is not the most comfortable environment for a nine-month-old baby."

She glared up at him, her slight body stiff with displeasure. "Only in your rarified environment could someone label this two-bedroom suite a mere hotel room. Many people raise their children in apartments smaller than this."

"I am not one of those many people and there is no reason for my son to be cramped here when there is a perfectly good villa in Greece childproofed and arranged for his comfort."

"I'd planned to do more Christmas shopping while we were here."

Memories of his step-aunt's excesses bombarded him. "Surely the past four days have been sufficient time to buy all you were going to buy...even for the most voracious shopper."

Her lips pursed, as if his words had offended. "You

might be surprised by this, but I've had too much on my mind the past few days to go shopping."

"You want me to believe you were so worried about me that you refrained from the delights of the shopping Mecca that is New York?"

"I don't expect you to believe anything good about me. You haven't so far." She turned away and started walking toward the door. "I'll fly home with your family. Heaven knows you didn't show a marked preference for my company before you forgot who I was and became convinced I am evil incarnate. It would be ludicrous to think you'd discover an untapped desire to be with me now."

He grabbed her shoulders and stopped her from leaving. Spinning her around to face him, he asked, "And why did I not like spending time with you?"

"I didn't say you didn't *like* to be with me."

"You said—"

"That you didn't show a *marked preference* for my company. It's not the same thing. Your business has always come first."

"You are sure it is not because I had a wife that made life away from home preferable to life at home?"

She twisted from his grip. "Believe what you like."

Damn it. Why did she have to sound so disheartened, like his awareness of her mercenary nature really hurt her?

She turned at the door to the bedroom, her eyes filled with sadness. "In answer to your question…I would say it's pretty obvious you found life at home boring or unpalatable, maybe even both. If you didn't, you would have spent more time there."

* * *

"You look pensive, Son. What are you thinking?"

Aristide looked up at his mother. Phillippa's beautiful brown eyes were fixed on him with obvious concern.

A striking woman, she was young enough to raise eyebrows when she announced the fact she was a grandmother. It was no surprise to him that she had finally remarried. The surprise had been that it had taken her so long.

She had been much younger than his father and still in her prime when Eugenios died. Yet, she had loved him so much that it had been more than a decade after his death before she accepted another man into her life. Aristide doubted she ever would have if she had not met Rachel's father. Vincent had been so obviously wounded by the years spent searching for his daughter that Phillippa's tender heart had been moved. First to compassion, and then to a love so genuine no one would ever deny its existence.

"I do not like this inability I have to remember my wife."

"No, of course not. Your amnesia is very difficult on both of you."

"So everyone keeps saying."

She reached out and squeezed his hand. "And we are all right. You hate to acknowledge weakness of any kind, but I know you must be very frightened by these holes in your memory."

He didn't want to dwell on his infirmity. He could not change it, therefore he would ignore it.

There were other matters of far more interest to him. "Was my marriage everything it should be?"

His mother's eyes widened in shock and then narrowed with an emotion he could not quite decipher. "Why would you ask me such a thing?"

"Doctor Lewis believes I had a reason for forgetting her. I am wondering if you know what it is."

"Eden is a good wife." His mother's staunch support of her daughter by marriage did not surprise him.

She was like a mama lion with her cub when it came to Rachel. He had no doubt that same attitude had prevailed with Eden upon his marriage, but he needed honesty, not platitudes given as a result of blind loyalty.

"Please, Mama, this is important."

Phillippa sighed, looking very uncomfortable and convincing him she knew more than she wanted to say. "Did you ask Eden?"

"She says she thinks I was not ready for marriage, that I forgot her because I never wanted the commitment to begin with."

"That is ridiculous." His mother's voice was laced with outrage. "No son of mine would be so weak!"

"I agree."

"But…" His mother's mouth drew down in a frown and she bit her lip as if trying to decide whether or not to remain silent.

"Tell me."

"Neither you nor Eden ever expressed dissatisfaction with your marriage. You must understand this."

"Your caveat is duly noted."

She accepted his words with a regal nod. "I am not certain how best to say this, but there were times I believed you were naïvely complacent."

"Me…not Eden?"

"Yes, you."

For some inexplicable reason the confirmation of his wife's unsuitability shocked him to the core, particularly coming from his mother. "What exactly are you saying?"

"You asked me if your marriage was all that it should be and I must tell you that many times I suspected it was not."

"Did I marry her to secure my place in Theo's life?"

"I often worried that was a larger part of your decision to marry than it should be. I had always hoped there was more genuine affection between you, but I did not pry."

"Did we seem affectionate?"

"You are a very private person, Aristide, even more so than your older brother. I have always found it difficult to read your emotions."

"In other words, there was no evidence of affection between the two of us."

"I did not say that. You men…you are always so literal and jump to conclusions all too easily. Your father was the same way."

Vincent arrived with a cup of tea for Phillippa and Aristide left off his questions. As she'd pointed out, he was private, too much so to discuss his marriage in front of the other man.

Eden waited for Aristide's plane to land, her nerves stretched so tight that she felt like a rubber band ready to snap. It had only lasted a few days, but this separation had been the worst one of her marriage—maybe because she had never felt less sure of what to expect upon her husband's return. Had he remembered anything of her at all? Surely he would have called to tell her if he had.

Beyond her uncertainty was a feeling of missing him that went bone deep. Unlike every other trip he'd taken away from her, Aristide had not called several times a day simply to connect and see how she and Theo were doing. She'd missed those calls terribly.

And it was as she realized just how aching her loneliness without him was that she asked herself how she could ever have contemplated divorce. How could she live the rest of her life without him when a mere three days without him had been such misery?

Would she have a choice?

The fear that she wouldn't was paramount.

He had not called at all except to say he would be flying in this evening. Apparently, he'd managed to wrap his meetings up with the help of his super-efficient assistant. She could only be grateful he had not delegated the telephone call to Kassandra.

Eden still smarted from the fact that he had sent her away and kept Kassandra by his side.

She thought maybe she understood his decision better after spending several sleepless hours analyzing the latest development in her marriage and coming to seriously regret her rejection of his sexual advances.

For Aristide, sex was as necessary as breathing, but he also had a strong sense of personal honor, not to mention a lion's dose of pride. Once she refused to make love to him, she should have realized he would see no recourse but to send her away. His desire for her was as strong as ever and he would have considered her too much of a temptation if she stayed. With the moratorium she had placed on sex, her presence in his bed would constitute a risk to both his pride and sense of self-control.

Eden wished she'd taken that into account before leaving the playing field wide open to her rival, but she hadn't been thinking all that clearly at the time. She'd been reacting.

Even more important than the fact that her denial had probably been what incited him to send her back to Greece ahead of time, she now wondered if he would regain his memory if she allowed him to make love to her. It was the one aspect of their marriage they always got right and, if they made love, it would have to prove to him that she was not the monster wife he suspected.

In addition, they communicated more between the sheets than anywhere else and she would have done well to remember that salient fact. It was the one place he never stinted on showing her affection or telling her how much he needed her. They'd been in bed together when he asked her to marry him. He'd told her about the effect of his father's death on him, how his uncle's painful marriage had impacted Aristide and the rest of the family and his pleasure in Phillippa's newfound happiness all during discussions post-coitus.

She couldn't believe she hadn't thought of it before, but by refusing to make love with him, she was denying the biggest catalyst she could give him for remembering her.

She'd decided to pick him up from the airport personally and planned to tell him she wanted to be a proper wife to him again on the drive home. Phillippa and Vincent were staying at the villa. Eden's best opportunity for a private, uninterrupted conversation with Aristide was now. Between Theo's needs, the servants who were ever present and a very concerned mother-in-law, her chances of being alone with Aristide were extremely slim.

Phillippa had told Eden that Aristide had asked his mother about their marriage. That showed more than anything that her husband was full of confusion and doubt. Acknowledging his own ignorance of their relationship would have been hard for the proud man she had married.

Interestingly, Phillippa had told her son that she thought he'd been blindly complacent in his marriage. Eden appreciated the sentiment. Aristide had assumed her love meant she would put up with anything.

He had never realized how much his lack of commitment to spending significant time with her had hurt her or taken stock of the damage it was doing to their marriage. Nor had he ever stopped to wonder why Eden frequently refused to attend social functions when she knew Kassandra would be present.

While they couldn't discuss any of these things until he remembered her, she was determined to do so as soon after he regained his memory as possible. Not only that, but she'd spoken to Adam on the phone just that day and the doctor had once again reiterated that it would be better to wait to tell Aristide of her current pregnancy.

In one respect, she had no problem with that. She wanted her husband's honest reaction to her and didn't think she'd get it if he knew she was pregnant again. Just as he had hidden his lack of any real desire to marry in the first place because of Theo. But in another respect, she desperately wanted to share news of the child growing inside her.

Sharing her first pregnancy with Aristide had been really special and there was a craven part of her that just wanted to go back to a time when he treated her so tenderly.

No matter what way she looked at it, his selective amnesia had effectively put their marriage on hold and the situation was intolerable. If it meant making love to a man who saw her as little more than a stranger so her husband could regain his memory and they could move forward, then she was prepared to do it.

"Eden. What are you doing here? Where is Aldo?" Aristide's tone was no more welcoming than his words, but she'd been expecting that reaction and forced herself not to take offence.

"I cancelled the car and came instead. You used to say you'd like it very much if I met you at the airport."

He'd implied he wouldn't mind making love in the limo on the way home because he was so hungry for her. She wasn't ready for that and she hadn't brought the limo, but she was hoping neither fact would matter since he would have no way of remembering his teasing.

"Did I?"

"Uh…huh. Anyway, I thought we could talk while I drove you home."

"I will do the driving," he said arrogantly.

"I hope you brought the Mercedes," Kassandra inserted from where she stood behind him. "After two weeks in New York, I have extra luggage."

Eden bit back a grimace, realizing her tactical blunder only at that moment. What an idiot she'd been. She'd been so wrapped up in thoughts of her marriage she'd actually managed to forget all about the other woman. Only Kassandra would of course have expected to ride home in the car chauffeured by Aldo as well.

"I'm surprised you didn't have your purchases shipped," Eden said by way of hiding her chagrin.

"There was no time." Kassandra smiled sweetly at her boss. "Aristide took me shopping and we didn't get done until a short time before takeoff."

Eden couldn't help flinching at the words, even knowing any sign of upset would give the Greek woman a great deal of satisfaction. She'd wanted to do her final Christmas shopping in New York with Aristide, but he'd turned her down, even though he clearly had found shopping with Kassandra no hardship.

"I brought the Jaguar." She bit her lip and looked at Aristide, mentally pleading for his understanding. "I thought you might insist on driving and you have always preferred it."

His frown said he wasn't impressed by her reasoning. "That's a small car to transport three people."

He was right. The car's backseat wasn't designed for luggage, it was miniscule, especially to a woman of Kassandra's height. The trunk wasn't much better. "Maybe Kassandra would be more comfortable taking a taxi to her apartment where there will be plenty of room for her bags."

The Greek woman made a moue of distaste. "If I had known you were going to change the transport arrangements I made, I would have had a car waiting to pick me up, but I suppose there's nothing for it than to wait in a taxi queue."

"Nonsense. Since Eden made the change, I am sure she will not mind waiting here while I run you home."

Eden opened her mouth to tell them both what they could do with their assumption that her needs always came last, but then snapped it shut. Kassandra was obviously hoping for just such a reaction and then she would undoubtedly offer to take a taxi again and Aristide would think Eden was acting the bitch.

Once again, she hadn't considered all the angles before acting. She had wanted to please Aristide by bringing his favorite car, but she had also wanted the increased intimacy in the atmosphere of the Jaguar over the Mercedes. She had completely forgotten about the need to see Kassandra home and thereby shot herself in the foot.

However, no way was she going to cool her heels at the airport while he and Kassandra took off together. "Don't be silly. You don't want to have to drive all the way back to the airport from Kassandra's apartment before going home. I'm small and will fit in the backseat, even with an extra piece of luggage or two."

She turned and headed toward the car before either of her nemeses could argue.

CHAPTER SIX

EDEN WAS feeling slightly better after they dropped Kassandra off.

The other woman had attempted to cut Eden out of the conversation in the car, but this time it had been Aristide himself who foiled her ploy. He had asked numerous questions about Theo and the rest of the family that Eden answered with enthusiasm.

"Did the meetings go well?" she asked as he pulled away from Kassandra's home.

"As you heard."

So much for that topic. "I did a lot of thinking while you were gone."

"And did this thinking lead anywhere productive?"

"I believe so."

"Enlighten me."

"It occurred to me that I made a mistake refusing to make love to you in New York. I was being overly sensitive."

He tensed, his expression turning stoic in a way she'd always hated. It shut her out. "On the contrary," he said, "sex between us right now would be nonproductive."

"Nonproductive?" She couldn't believe what she was hearing.

His jaw set with granitelike hardness. "I've decided to move into a guest room for the time being."

"A guest room?"

"Do you plan to repeat everything I say from here on out?" he responded coldly.

"No." She forced her thoughts into working order so she didn't do it again, but flabbergasted didn't begin to describe the way she felt at his announcement. "Your mother and Vincent are staying at the villa."

"And?"

"Are you prepared to answer questions from her about why you are sleeping in a guest room?"

"I have no doubt she will understand."

"Before or after you explain it?" she asked helplessly.

"Does it matter?"

"No, I guess not." Not if he was willing to make the explanations. To her way of thinking, that little fact was as significant as the move itself. She shook her head, trying to clear it. He really was rejecting her sexually. She couldn't believe it. "But celibacy is not your style."

"I am not such a Neanderthal that I would insist on claiming my marital rights with a woman I do not remember marrying merely to satisfy my sexual urges."

"Maybe you plan to satisfy them elsewhere," she accused with pain-filled uncertainty. She knew only one thing for sure—her husband was less acquainted with sexual denial than he was with being poor.

"What the hell are you talking about?"

"You told me in New York that you didn't feel married. Does that mean you don't feel bound by your vow of fidelity? Not that you even said one," she rambled in confused shock, "the marriage ceremony in a judge's office is somewhat truncated."

"I do not intend to have sex with another woman."

"You expect me to believe you are willingly embracing celibacy for the indefinite future?"

"Why not? I travel quite a bit. I assume you would not have stayed married to a man who strayed." Sarcasm dripped off his tongue like acid.

"You assume correctly."

"I may not remember you, or our marriage, but I know myself and I would not have had sex with any woman but my wife."

"Are you sure about that? Kassandra's more than willing. She's made it clear to me that she's *eager* and, according to her, you're *already* lovers. Presumably, you would remember *that*, since you remember *her*."

"She told me you had jealous delusions about us."

"Did she?" Eden stared out the window, the darkened landscape not registering. "Which means what—you naturally assume I'm lying when I say she told me you two were lovers?"

She could feel him looking at her, but she refused to return his regard. She couldn't quite bounce back from a rejection she had never expected. The one thing she'd been certain of in her marriage to Aristide was his desire for her. She'd doubted his emotional attachment, but never his physical need. Now he was saying he didn't need her.

Was he having an affair with Kassandra? She had to contemplate the possibility his decision to move into a guest room reflected a turn of events she would have given almost anything not to face.

"When are you alleging Kassandra told you this?"

She tensed at his choice of words, a familiar sense of impotent anger surging up inside of her. "I'm not alleging anything. I'm stating a fact. She was waiting for me when

I came out of your hospital room the day before you were discharged. We argued."

"And she told you we are lovers?" he asked, sounding disbelieving.

"Not exactly."

"Ah…"

She turned her head and looked at him then. His focus was on the road ahead, but she knew his peripheral vision was superior and she gave him a hot glare.

"Kassandra asked me point-blank if I was sure you weren't lovers. If that isn't an implication the two of you are having an affair, I don't know what is."

"Is that why you slapped her?"

"No." She opened her mouth to add more, but didn't know what to say.

Kassandra had been careful to lace her threats with innuendo. Repeating the conversation verbatim would not convince Aristide that Eden had been justified in her reaction. He would have had to have been there…and inside her heart, dealing with her pain to understand it.

And what were the chances Aristide would even begin to believe his precious Kassandra was intentionally undermining his marriage? Before the accident, they had been slim, but now that he didn't remember Eden or trust her at all, they were nonexistent.

Silence fell between them as she went back to looking out the window.

"Are you going to tell me why you did slap her?"

"I see no point in doing so."

"If it is something I need to discuss with her…"

"You've already made it clear who you blame for that altercation and it isn't your assistant."

"Maybe I did not have all the facts."

"It wouldn't make any difference if you did. You would still blame me because while you'll bend over backwards to give her the benefit of the doubt, you assume the worst about me and have done since waking up from your coma. I'm your wife, but you didn't stand by me and there's really nothing else to say in the face of that."

"Kassandra was there for me in the hospital when you were not. She is a devoted employee as well as a long-time friend. I would be a fool to trust the word of a woman I cannot remember over hers. After all, I did not wake from my coma having wiped *her* entirely from my brain. And I have to question why that was."

Pain ripped through Eden like a hurricane and she felt as ravaged as any debris-strewn coastline. She swallowed convulsively, her throat tight with tears. Because he hadn't just forgotten her, he'd forgotten their unborn baby as well. Somehow that made it ten times worse.

Not only had he obviously subconsciously wanted to wipe her existence in his life, but he'd also wanted to forget the tie an additional child between them would forge.

From the moment she had woken up in the hospital after the accident, she had been determined to fight for her marriage. Why? Because she loved Aristide so much she thought she might die inside without him. But he was tearing her heart to shreds and if she wasn't *dying* right now, she was certainly hurting.

Maybe it was time she faced that her love meant nothing in the face of his indifference.

What that meant for her future, for the future of her children and their life with her and their father, she didn't even want to contemplate. But one thing she knew—her hope was a dead weight in her chest, along with her leaden heart.

* * *

When they reached the villa, she left him to look in on Theo while she began moving his things from the master suite to a guest room down the hall. By the time he walked in forty-five minutes later, she and a maid had cleared out his dresser and most of his wardrobe.

He had his suitcase in his hand when he walked in. "What the hell is going on in here?"

"You're in the room at the end of the hall." She looked pointedly at his suitcase.

The maid came out of the walk-in closet carrying a big armful of his suits. Eden stepped out of the way so she could leave the room.

Aristide wasn't so obliging. "Where are you taking my things?" he asked in a dangerously soft voice.

The maid flinched, but Eden wasn't bothered by her husband's apparent anger. She was only doing what he wanted, after all.

"She's taking your suits to your new room."

"My new room?"

Now who was repeating words? "Yes. We're almost done moving you. I'll just transfer your things from our…I mean *my* bathroom and you'll be all settled in."

"I did not intend to move completely out of *our* bedroom."

"You'll be sleeping in another room, right?"

"For the time being."

"I'm sure you'll be more comfortable not having to go searching for your things between there and here…"

She'd never seen Aristide look lost for words, not in all the time she'd known him. She would have laughed if she wasn't hurting so much. He looked royally flummoxed now and that gave her a sense of grim satisfaction. He'd been standing her world on its ear since the day they met.

It was time she turned the tables a bit.

"If you will excuse me, I'll just collect your gear from the *en suite*."

"Damn it, Eden!"

"What is happening?" Phillippa stood in the doorway, her face creased with concern. "I saw the maid carrying Aristide's clothing into another room."

"Your son has decided he feels more comfortable sleeping elsewhere…for the time being. He seems to think you'll understand and no explanations are necessary. Should he be wrong, I suggest you ask him about it. He also made it clear he doesn't mind explaining if the need should arise."

Aristide watched as his wife spun on her heel and marched into the *en suite*.

His mother gasped. "Aristide?" she asked uncertainly.

"Yes?"

"Eden…"

"Has taken my desire to sleep in separate quarters at present to mean I no longer belong in our bedroom."

Her words to his mother had been filled with bitterness, but her eyes had reflected a pain that tore at something deep inside him. Did she think he didn't want her? Nothing could be further from the truth, but their relationship was too muddled as it was to confuse with sex. They both needed this time of adjustment.

From the expression on her face when she'd walked away, she didn't see it that way though. She was taking his desire to sleep in another bed as a form of rejection…one he had never intended. His usually superior brain had let him down when he assumed she would understand something he barely understood himself.

He cursed again and earned a censorious frown from his mother.

"You told her you wanted to sleep in a separate bed?" she asked, as if trying to take in a very shocking turn of events.

"*Ohi*," he affirmed.

She shook her head. "That was stupid."

"There is enough confusion in our situation right now. We do not need it clouded with sex."

She stared at him like she doubted his sanity or intelligence, or maybe even both.

This was not a conversation he wanted to have with his mother. "My decision is not up for discussion."

"Do not take that tone with me, Aristide."

"I apologize if my tone was disrespectful, but you must allow me to handle my marriage as I see fit."

"The problem is that you are not handling it, my son. You are undermining it when you can least afford to do so. Know this, Aristide—if you mess up your marriage, you will have no one to blame but yourself." With that, she turned and left the room.

Aristide felt like he'd stepped into an alternate dimension where everyone but him knew the rules. In New York, his mother had as good as said Eden wasn't the wife she should have been and now she was thrusting the blame for any failure in his marriage squarely on his shoulders.

His head began to ache again.

Eden came out of the bathroom, her arms laden with his toiletries. "I'll just drop these off in your bathroom."

Even though she had been the one to initially say she did not want to make love while he could not remember her, rejected hurt emanated from her every lovely pore. Clearly, she had changed her mind and did not appreciate the fact that he now questioned the wisdom of sharing a bed.

However, instead of arguing his decision to sleep elsewhere like he would have expected from her reaction, she was intent on removing every trace of his occupancy from their bedroom.

The sense of foreboding that hovered around the edges of his marriage increased until he felt suffocated by it. "This is not necessary."

"I don't agree."

Desperation seared through him and fear clouded his thoughts until he was on the verge of recanting his desire to sleep in another bed. She didn't give him the chance, but marched from the room.

"Eden!" he called after her, that incomprehensible desperation lacing his voice.

Could she hear it? If she did, she ignored it as she continued down the hall as if he had never spoken.

He opened his mouth to demand she come back and then snapped it shut again. This was stupid. These feelings tormenting him were irrational and he would not be dictated to by them. He was stronger than that.

But he didn't feel strong…he felt like he was making a major tactical error here. Sleeping elsewhere had seemed so logical when he had been considering how to handle his aching desire for a woman he could not remember. He had to wonder if he'd been thinking straight.

Or was the problem that he was confused now? His usually superior brain felt like mush. His pride barely allowed him to acknowledge his possible mistake to himself, but no way could he admit it to *her*.

So there was nothing for it but to make his way to the guest room down the hall. It did not escape his notice that the bedroom was the furthest she could get him from the master suite without putting him in a different section of the villa entirely.

She walked out of the *en suite* as he entered the room. "You should be all set. Petra will unpack your case for you during dinner."

"Is that not a wife's job?"

"I don't think so," she mocked. "Besides, how can you have a wife if you don't feel like a husband?"

Eden hadn't been consciously baiting her husband, but as she watched the fireworks explode in his vibrant blue eyes, she realized this was exactly the reaction she'd been pushing for.

Something had snapped inside of her when he had told her so calmly that he wanted to sleep somewhere besides their bed. Coming from a man like Aristide, it was the ultimate rejection and she had been determined he feel at least the edge of its bite as well. And he had.

He didn't like having his things removed from their bedroom. It stung his pride and he deserved it. He'd lacerated hers along with her heart.

"Are you trying to imply you feel free to behave as if you are not married?" he asked in a deadly voice.

"No more than you do." He could take that any way he liked.

His eyes narrowed. He got it all right. "You do not think I take my vows seriously…you implied as much in the car."

She shrugged. "You said you weren't sleeping with Kassandra." Once. He'd said it once.

"But you do not believe me."

"I didn't say that."

Steel manacles masquerading as masculine fingers clamped down on her shoulders while rage vibrated around her. "But you think it, do you not? You believe I am having an affair with my assistant and for this reason, you think you have the right to similarly forget your promise of fidelity."

"We didn't make those promises at our wedding." And she was just now realizing how much she hated that, how she had felt slighted being married in a register office instead of a church.

"In Greece such promises are not part of the wedding ceremony. They are taken for granted."

"I wouldn't know. We had a ten-minute civil ceremony in New York. It was all the time you and my father could squeeze from your busy schedules."

"Surely not."

She sighed, the tension draining from her, leaving her exhausted in both body and spirit. "You left for a trip to England that night and he went back to the office after taking us out for a celebratory lunch."

"My mother would never have approved a register-office marriage."

"She didn't, but after you informed her I was already two months pregnant, she understood."

"I am sure she was ecstatic at the prospect of being a grandmother so quickly after our marriage."

"She made a few comments about neither of her sons seeming to get the whole 'first comes marriage and then comes babies' thing right, but, yes, she was very happy to have another grandchild on the way."

He was silent for a moment, seemingly letting go of his own nearly incandescent anger. "You did not realize you were pregnant immediately?" he asked, sounding wary.

"I figured it out within days of missing my period. I'm disgustingly regular in that department."

"Why did you wait to tell me?"

Funny how he just assumed she had, not that he had waited to marry her. It irked her that she could not fault him on that score. Right now, she wanted to fault him on everything, she was hurting so much.

"I didn't have a choice," she admitted. "You were in Greece and it wasn't something I was going to tell you over the phone."

"I spend more than half of my life in New York. You expected my imminent return," he correctly guessed. "We met there?"

"Yes. I was in town visiting my dad. We met outside the Metropolitan Museum of Art. I was planning to take in an exhibit while Dad was in a meeting and you were headed to lunch with someone else. You cancelled and spent the afternoon with me instead."

It had shocked and delighted her that he had acted as affected by her as she had been by him. It had taken her a while to realize her effect on him was mainly sexual while he had come to dominate her heart, her body and her thoughts.

"You said you were visiting your father? You did not live in New York?"

She shook her head. "I lived in a small town upstate. That's where we were headed when we were hit by the truck."

"You feel badly about this?"

He knew her better than he should, considering she was nothing but a stranger to him. "Yes. If we had stayed in the city, the accident would not have happened."

"These things happen. It was not your fault."

He was wrong. Her bombshell had been just that, even though she'd convinced herself that her asking for a divorce would hardly impact him. If he, or their baby, had died because of her poor timing, she would never have forgiven herself.

His vibrant blue eyes narrowed. "We live in Greece."

She knew what he was asking without him saying the words. Why not New York when he spent so much time there? "You wanted your children raised in your home country," she said.

His brow creased. "I've decreased my trips to New York in the last year or so."

Not enough, but, "Yes."

"I am *not* having an affair with Kassandra."

"But you have had." She'd always suspected, but he'd refused to discuss it.

Never once had he denied that the two had slept together, but he'd been unwilling to talk about it if they had. And because she hadn't been sure that Kassandra was even sexually active, she hadn't pressed. Now she realized how silly she'd ever been to think the reason he had held himself back from the woman was because of her innocence.

Kassandra was as innocent as a viper.

"My relationships before I met you are not up for discussion."

"So you've said before, but are you so sure your relationship with *her* ended *before* we met?"

"When did we meet?"

"Almost three years ago."

The look of confused uncertainty on his face was like taking a rapier thrust to the heart.

"You were lovers, weren't you? And you can't be sure it ended before we met because the timing was that close, wasn't it?"

He let her go with the speed of a snake retreating and

stepped back. "This conversation is pointless, you know I can't remember."

"How convenient."

"Do you think I do not want to answer you?"

"You said earlier that you know yourself well and that you would not sleep with a woman besides your wife, but your uncertainty now undermines that assertion, don't you think?"

He rubbed his forehead with his thumb and forefinger. "No, damn it. I know I would never respect myself if I had an affair when I was married."

"Which does not preclude you having her as your lover at the same time you were seeing me. After all, our relationship was hardly a committed one, no matter what daydreams I wove around you at the time."

"What do you mean?" he asked, his tension palpable.

"We were together well over a year before I got pregnant and you never once asked me to Greece to meet your family. Heck, you didn't even invite me to have dinner with you and your brother when he was in town. There were times I felt like your dirty secret and the funny thing is, before I met you, I would have said I would give a guy a verbal kick in the teeth for treating me that way."

He'd certainly changed after their marriage, insisting she meet everyone from the receptionist at Kouros Industries' headquarters to his second cousin who lived in Turkey. But privately she'd always wondered if that had been for the sake of their baby, or for her. He had been so proud about his first foray into fatherhood.

"Your other lovers all took you home to meet their parents?" he asked cynically.

"There were no other lovers. Sex was never a casual thing for me. I planned to wait until I got married."

"Are you implying I seduced you?"

"Is it seduction when a woman has no thought of saying no?" She sighed. "This is getting us nowhere."

She turned and headed for the door. "I'll see you at dinner."

"Eden."

She stopped with her hand on the doorframe. "What?"

"You are my wife now."

"So the certificate in your study says."

"It is more than a piece of paper...*I am your husband*."

She looked back over her shoulder, taking in his ferocious tension.

She indicated the room with a sweep of her hand. "As you said to me in the hospital...the evidence is not in your favor."

CHAPTER SEVEN

"I AM SURPRISED you let Eden stray so far from your side."
The deep male voice belonged to Aristide's business associate and friend, Leiandros Kiriakis.

Aristide gritted his teeth against making an irritated retort and forced himself to face the other man with an expression of equanimity. "Leiandros, it is good to see you."

"You have recently returned from New York, have you not?"

"A week ago."

"Then I am doubly surprised Eden is more than six inches from your side. That is unlike you."

Was the other man implying that Aristide usually hung around his wife like a lost puppy? The image did not sit well and he frowned.

He had made the choice not to share his amnesia with anyone but family, so he could not expect a tactful handling of anomalies in his demeanor toward Eden. And, being honest with himself, he had to admit his annoyance did not stem from Leiandros noting the strange behavior anyway. It resulted from the fact that Eden had been *straying from Aristide's side* since the night she'd moved him out of their bedroom.

She had closed herself off from him, maintaining a definite emotional distance and going so far as to create a physical one when possible as well. She avoided sharing any meal but dinner with him and then she barely spoke to him. And she only tolerated his nightly presence during Theo's bath time because she wanted their son to maintain his sense of security. She had as much as told Aristide so.

He hadn't realized how much of herself she had left open to him until her manner had altered so significantly. Even having only the short time in New York and the drive from the airport to compare it to, her change toward him was so marked, he could not mistake it.

And while she was busy ignoring him, he was fully occupied trying to interpret the reaction of his family and others toward Eden. Their staff adored his rather quiet wife and, regardless of what she had implied about their marriage in New York, his mother treated Eden with a great deal of affection. It was nothing like the way she had reacted to Andrea Demakis. And Rachel was just as accepting of her sister-in-law.

Vincent and Sebastian's attitude toward Aristide's wife was one of warm indulgence. He would not have said either man was easily fooled, but Eden might be the consummate actress.

Not only that, but his own pride could well have spurred him to act like he was happy in his marriage no matter what had brought it about. Three irrefutable facts kept him wary toward his tempting little wife. One, even Eden admitted he had married her because she was pregnant. She claimed it had not been a trap, but she would hardly say anything else.

Two, he had forgotten her and all the research he had done on his condition pointed to the probability he had forgotten her because he subconsciously wanted or needed to. And three, she wielded power over his libido and emotions that no other woman ever had. That made her dangerous. Strong evidence of that fact was that, no matter how wary he felt toward her, Eden's current attempt to hold him at a distance really bothered him.

"Aristide?" Leiandros looked concerned.

Well he might. Aristide was staring across the room like a man in a trance. His pride balked at the picture he made.

"She is enjoying herself," he said, trying to explain his own apparently unusual behavior and save face.

She stood on the other side of the room, laughing with a group of *his* friends, yet they were people that knew her infinitely better than he did because of his memory loss. That knowledge brought him an unpleasant sensation of jealousy.

"No doubt, but I would say you are not, my friend." The knowing in Leiandros's eyes was as bad as being with his brother, Sebastian.

The shipping tycoon was older than both Aristide and Sebastian, but they'd been friends for years. There weren't that many men in the world, much less Greece, with the power, the wealth or the inner drive that all three possessed.

Even fewer that held and therefore practiced their particular stand on business ethics. It was no surprise the three men were friends despite the slight age difference, but the fact that they functioned so well in the business arena together shocked many.

"*I am fine.* Where is Savannah?" Aristide asked to change the subject.

His friend's features softened. "She and the children are shopping for my Christmas present. I am not allowed to see it, so I have been banished. She promised to join me here as soon as she settled the children with my mother."

"You didn't wait to come with her?"

"You know how it is…there are always business discussions at a gathering like this. I want to get them out of the way before my wife arrives, so she can command my full attention."

"You two are very devoted." There had been a lot of gossip when Leiandros married his cousin's widow, but even the most determined naysayers did not question the couple's deep and loving affection now.

"As are you and Eden."

"Do you think so?"

Leiandros's expression sharpened. "Definitely, but why would you ask such a thing?"

He shrugged. He could hardly tell the other man he couldn't remember his wife and therefore had no idea what sort of relationship they had before. From what Leiandros implied, either Aristide had been very good at putting on a front, or his relationship with Eden was not the unequal and unhappy union the facts of his present condition implied. He was fairly certain it had been nothing like the armed truce they were currently engaged in either.

Tired of that truce and the amalgam of unnamed needs that swirled through him constantly when it came to his wife, Aristide took leave of his friend.

He stopped beside Eden and laid his arm over her shoulders. It felt right and she smelled so damn good. It was a scent, like springtime after a rain, that he did not associate with anyone else. Her soft skin tantalized his fingertips and he could not help brushing his thumb along her exposed shoulder.

His friends apparently found nothing odd in this gesture of affection, none of them so much as blinking, but his wife went as stiff as a board beside him. She made a subtle effort to shrug off his hand, but rather than let her go, he pulled her closer. He knew it was a mistake the second he did it as a sexual charge leapt through his body and he became instantly aroused.

He had been an idiot to deny himself the pleasure of intimacy with his wife.

Doing his best to control a libido rapidly spiraling out of control, he smiled down at her. "Enjoying yourself?"

Her lips curved in an answering gesture that did not begin to reach her vulnerable gray eyes. "Yes, of course. I've been looking forward to this party for weeks."

The hostess, who was in the group surrounding Eden, looked pleased. "You did a lot to help me plan it."

The party was more than a gathering of friends for the holidays. It was a fund raiser for a worldwide children's organization. That much he remembered.

But Eden had helped plan it? That was hardly the action of a woman who had trapped him into marriage for mercenary motives.

"And you are pleased with the results?" he asked, his heart rate increasing as Eden's scent continued to tease his senses.

He could feel himself growing hard and changed his stance with Eden so she stood partially in front of him.

Apparently unaware of his predicament, the hostess nodded enthusiastically. "We raised over one hundred thousand dollars."

"That's fantastic!" Eden said, relaxing, her pleasure in the success of the evening blatant and clearly genuine.

He could not remember if he had donated anything beyond the door admission for him and his wife. Couldn't even remember buying the tickets. His mother and brother were here as well, but he didn't know if they had bought their own tickets. He hated these lapses of knowledge in his memory.

The hostess laughed. "How could it be anything else? You bought tickets for so many people here, Eden, it should be your name being bandied about tonight, not mine."

Well that answered one question…the one of who had bought the tickets. It was such a small thing, but there were so many little glitches like that in his memory banks, they were driving him crazy. His personal frustration aside, he could not fault a wife who had used his resources in such a fashion.

"Like I had anything else to do with my allowance," Eden said, sounding very American. "Aristide is so generous with me, I never have to buy anything for myself."

The unexpected approval in her voice warmed him. Until he remembered that approval was for the man he'd been before he lost his memory. She certainly wasn't as enamored of the man he was now…or at least the way that man treated her.

"I would happily double your allowance if this is how you would like to spend the money," he said honestly.

She looked up at him, her expression open and filled with pleasure for the first time in days. "Are you serious?"

"Very." He would triple it, if doing so would keep that expression on her face when she looked at him. "In fact, I will put you in charge of Kouros Industries' charitable contributions if you like."

Her expression closed up immediately and she looked away, all the relaxing her body had done disappearing in the blink of an eye. "That is Kassandra's domain."

"She has enough to keep her busy, she will be content to give that up, I am sure."

"Don't bet on it," Eden muttered.

"It does not matter. I am the boss, not she."

Eden's snort was followed by good-natured laughter from those around him. Clearly, the others thought she was teasing him, but he knew better.

He turned her to face him, his already overactive libido going into overdrive as he got a very nice view down the front of her slinky little dress. Damn it. Had other men seen her this way tonight? He could see the top swell of her breasts and it didn't take much imagination to picture her nipples a little further down.

His sex tightened and he had to bite back a groan. He wanted her with an obsessive ache that grew with every passing day.

"You mock me at your peril," he growled with a teasing look for the benefit of the others.

She gave him a saucy grin that went straight to his groin. "What are you going to do about it?"

He knew what he wanted to do about it, but making love to her in front of an audience was not exactly his thing. "Wait until we get home and see," he threatened.

Her eyes widened with mock trepidation and something else he could swear was very real anticipation.

Something flashed in his head…an impression, if not a clear memory. This type of teasing between them was not a new thing and it had been something he had enjoyed a great deal.

"The way you two carry on, it's hard to understand how you can stand to live apart as much as you do," their hostess said with a laugh.

The animation and anticipation drained out of Eden as if it had never been there. Reality flooded back. She stepped away before he could stop her. "You know what Aristide always says, it keeps our relationship fresh."

He didn't know how he had looked at things before, but more time spent together now would reveal her true nature faster than their current living arrangement. "Theo is older and he made the last trip to New York as if he was born to air travel. There is no reason you cannot travel with me now."

A mysterious shadow passed through her gray eyes, but all she did was shrug.

"You always said having your wife along would be too much of a distraction, Aristide." Kassandra joined their small group, her smile directed at him.

He did not miss the way she effectively cut his wife without making a point of doing so. Was she being protective? She had implied she felt he needed it when it came to his wife. Even so, she could not be allowed to behave rudely toward Eden. He had chosen to marry her, and no matter how his loyal friend and employee felt about that, she needed to respect his decision.

"Maybe I have changed my mind."

"You no longer find Eden a distraction?" Kassandra asked, the barb so subtle he would have missed it but for the stonelike quality that took over his lovely wife's expression.

She was obviously very sensitive where his assistant was concerned. And he could not forget that she had accused the two of them of being lovers.

Kassandra had explained her remarks to Eden outside the hospital room, but his wife's ultra-sensitivity to the other woman would account for her taking them the opposite way they had been intended.

"On the contrary," he said for his wife's benefit, "I feel as if I've just gotten married for the first time again. If I can do my job while living with my wife in Greece, I fail to see how she would hamper me in New York or anywhere else for that matter."

Eden couldn't believe her ears. He was saying what she had thought for so long she almost pinched herself to see if she was in some bizarre dream.

"I do not know…I think marriage to a woman as delectable as your wife would be a constant distraction no matter where I lived and worked," an Italian man, who had joined their group just before Aristide, said.

She had never met him before, but the way he looked at her made her feel like crossing her arms over her less than generous curves.

"And you are?" Aristide asked with freezing cool that left no doubt what he thought of the other man's comment.

"Haven't you met Giuseppe?" their hostess asked, jumping in with an adroit maneuver meant to defuse the situation. "He's a great supporter of children's charities."

"Now that your husband is putting you in charge of corporate charities, we'll have to get together for lunch and talk over some of my pet projects." Giuseppe's sensual mouth curved in a smile that intimated he was interested in more than discussing their mutual interest in needy children.

She remembered someone saying once that all Italian men flirted, but she couldn't imagine most of them did it this blatantly. What did he see between her and Aristide that he thought he could get away with it or that she might possibly welcome it? Maybe it was the fact she had spent the first forty-five minutes of the party being virtually ignored by her tycoon spouse.

He wasn't ignoring her now though. Aristide looked ready to blow a gasket, but Kassandra's shocked gasp was audible to everyone.

"I thought you were happy with my management of that area of the company," she said, affecting a wounded attitude.

Eden nearly ground her teeth in frustration, certain Aristide's offer would be rescinded in days, if not hours. Kassandra was very adept at undermining Eden's progress with her husband.

"If you find you do not wish to alter your company's arrangements, I would be very happy to discuss Eden helping me with my efforts," Giuseppe said and Eden could have kissed him.

Their hostess smiled brightly, ignoring the undercurrents of the situation as any good society hostess would try to do. "What a wonderful idea."

"No, thank you," Aristide said to Giuseppe, shockingly talking right over their hostess's words. "My wife is sufficiently occupied. She does not have time to pursue outside endeavors of the type you are suggesting."

She should be used to having her sometimes arrogant Greek husband speak for her, but she wasn't and didn't plan to ever develop any real tolerance for it. "I think that is a decision I need to make, Aristide."

"Absolutely. You have got to remember, your wife is *American*." Kassandra said it like Eden was an alien species. "She prefers to remain independent in many ways. Playing the heavy husband will not go over well with her."

"When I need marital advice I will ask for it," Aristide said with a glacial look and more censure than Eden had ever heard him use toward his assistant.

Kassandra's big brown eyes filled with glistening moisture and her lip quivered. "Of course, I never meant… I know I am only your employee. If you will all excuse me." She spun on her heel and rushed toward the terrace.

Aristide cursed and, without consulting Eden, excused them both from the small group. He started tugging her toward the terrace, but she dug her heels in.

"Where do you think you're taking me?"

"I was rude and I need to apologize to her."

"You were honest."

"I hurt her."

"You hurt me, but I haven't received any heartfelt apologies."

The look of chagrin on his features said her words had hit their mark.

She pulled her arm from his grasp. "Go talk to her if you think you need to, but leave me out of it."

His hands fisted at his sides and his body went rigid with tension, but he nodded. "Perhaps that would be best."

Eden watched him walk away, her stomach churning and ended up making her own mad dash for the bathroom. Morning sickness that did not limit itself to the mornings was the pits. When she came out fifteen minutes later, Aristide and Kassandra were just returning from the terrace together.

Eden walked in the opposite direction the couple was heading. She'd had enough of her husband's assistant's company for one evening. She spent the next hour avoiding them both, catching a glimpse of irritation on her husband's face more than once when she made herself scarce the minute he walked into a room. Well, too bad.

She'd warned him her tolerance level for Kassandra's game playing was at an all-time low. He should have listened, but, unsurprisingly, he had chosen to dismiss her concerns.

She was in an animated discussion about children's charities with Sebastian, Rachel and Giuseppe when she sensed Aristide's presence behind her. A scant second later his arm landed around her shoulder and it was all she could do not to throw it off, but she felt they'd caused enough of a scene tonight.

"Your wife has a real admirer here, little brother," Sebastian said with more warning than teasing.

Eden frowned at her brother-in-law.

He grinned back at her, unrepentant. "You're a lovely woman, Eden…it is no surprise my brother is not the only man to appreciate you so enthusiastically."

Giuseppe smiled as well, his eyes roaming over her like hands. "You are a very lucky man, Signor Kouros."

Aristide went rigid beside her, his hold on her shoulder tightening almost painfully. "I am well aware of my good fortune in my choice of a wife."

The words were born of his pride, not honesty, and that infuriated her. Not only had he *not chosen* her for his wife—nature had done that for him in allowing her to become pregnant—but he could in no way imply he currently wanted to be her husband in any shape or form.

Angry at his willingness to claim her for the sake of his ego and not her heart, she twisted out of his hold. "I'm ready to go home."

"The evening is still young," Giuseppe said.

Almost as annoyed with the Italian as she was with Aristide, she smiled saccharine sweetly at him. "Then I suggest you find someone young to share it with you. As we say back home, I'm an old married woman. My baby son will wake me up bright and early no matter what time I go to sleep tonight."

She turned to Aristide. "You are welcome to stay. I can catch a taxi home with no trouble at all."

"We will drop you off," Sebastian said quickly. "Our little ones do not sleep much past dawn either, right, *agape mou*?" he asked, looking down at Rachel with love in his eyes.

Eden usually rejoiced in her in-laws' adoration for one another, but tonight it was like salt in a fresh wound. If she had to travel home, witnessing it at close proximity in the car, she would probably end up in tears and totally embarrassing herself.

"If you are ready to leave, I will of course accompany you," Aristide said with steel in his voice.

She had no desire to argue, but neither did she offer him any conversation once they were in the car. She could tell he was just sitting there stewing, his driving movement precise and indicative of tightly controlled anger.

They were almost to the villa when he broke the silence. "I do not appreciate my wife flirting with other men."

"I did not flirt."

"Giuseppe wants you."

"That's his problem."

"Is it?"

"Yes. I don't want him."

"Are you sure?"

"I'm a married woman, for heaven's sake, Aristide."

"But you do not feel like a married woman."

"That doesn't mean I'm going to jump in bed with the first beautiful Italian man who asks me." Giuseppe had been over the top and even a little smarmy in the way he looked at her, but he'd also been gorgeous.

His jaw clenched. "And if I asked you?"

"Asked me what?"

"To go to bed with me."

"After you disappeared on the terrace with your personal assistant?" She made a sound of disgust. "Forget it."

He said a very nasty American swear word. "She was

LUCY MONROE   111

upset. You told me to go to her. What did you expect me
to do, ignore her distress?"

"Why not? You've done a very good job of ignoring
mine on more than one occasion. And I didn't tell you to
go to her. I made it clear I wanted no part of it, if you did."

"I'm sorry if my actions tonight offended you." It was
a stilted apology at best.

"Celibacy starting to wear on you, is it?" she asked cynically, implying that was his only reason for saying he was
sorry. And maybe it was.

"*Yes*, but my apology was sincere. It was not my intention to put Kassandra's feelings above your own. I did not
seek her out merely to soothe her feelings, but also to
make it clear I do not appreciate being the center of an
emotional scene."

She could easily see him doing that, but it did not ne-
gate the other. "Her feelings do come first."

"I want *you*," he said in a driven tone.

It was quite the climb down for the man who had told
her he didn't want sex clouding their relationship.

"What happened to sex between us being *nonproductive*?"

"I am fast learning that living together in the same
house and not making love is impossible."

"So, I'm an addiction you can't break even if you don't
remember ever wanting anything more than my body?"

"I did not say that."

"Tell me, Aristide…who will be managing the corporate charitable gifts for Kouros Industries in the future?"

Two streaks of red slashed across the chiseled features
of his face and she had her answer before he spoke. "I did
not realize how attached to that aspect of her job Kassandra was when I made the offer."

"No, of course not."

"But you knew…apparently this has come up before," he had the gall to say with implied accusation.

Kassandra's effective negative publicity campaign at work again.

"Yes, it has, in fact—with the same results, I might add," she said defiantly. "Do remember who made the suggestion and that it was not me."

"The corporate charity fund is not the issue here and it has nothing to do with me wanting to take you to my bed."

"But it has a great deal to do with me not wanting to be there."

"I have got to hand it to you, Eden…you almost had me fooled. I was beginning to think there was not a mercenary bone in your body."

"And you see my desire to use my time promoting worthy charities as money grubbing?" she mocked, refusing to acknowledge the pain more accusations about her character caused her.

"No," he ground out. "I see you using your body as a bargaining chip in that light."

Was he really that dense? "Is that honestly what you think I'm doing, using my body for barter?"

"What else?"

"You don't think it might be natural for a wife to want nothing of intimacy with a husband who repeatedly puts his employee's wishes above her own?" Not to mention the fact he didn't remember her, but that was not the issue of paramount importance at the moment.

"That is ridiculous…the two do not coincide. Kassandra's pleasure in her job has nothing to do with your role as my wife. If you want to set up a charitable fund and administer it, I will be the biggest donor."

"If I said yes and invited you into my bed, then that really would make me the mercenary bitch you are so intent on believing me to be. No, thank you, Aristide. I would rather work with the somewhat smarmy Giuseppe."

"Do not try it." The deadly venom in his tone sent chills over her and she didn't argue the point.

She didn't want to work with Giuseppe anyway. The man might care about malnourished and undereducated children, but that couldn't make up for the fact he was so obviously interested in having an affair with a married woman.

Eden could never respect or be drawn to a man of that ilk, but she wasn't about to admit that truth to her husband. He deserved to sweat it out a little, like she'd been sweating his relationship with Kassandra since the beginning of their marriage.

CHAPTER EIGHT

EDEN FED Theo his breakfast with a heavy heart.

Once again she was questioning her judgment in rejecting her husband. Had she made yet another mistake, or had she saved herself heartache? The last two weeks had been hard, but last night had been emotionally devastating.

Because for a very short time, it was as if she had Aristide back and that had both elated and frightened her. She was safe when her heart was locked away behind a cold wall built by his rejection, but when the wall started to crack, she realized she could still bleed.

She'd read somewhere that sometimes love was not enough. Her mother's love had been more of a handicap to her happiness than an emotion so powerful it could make up for her father's lack. Eden was beginning to think she had made the same mistake in marrying a man who did not love her the way she loved him.

But if love was not enough…if their marriage had to end, what did that say for Theo and the baby growing in Eden's womb? She shuddered at the thought of tearing them away from a father who would love them in a way her own father had never doted on her. Could she justify destroying their happiness for the sake of her own feelings?

She was so lost in thought, she did not hear Aristide come into the kitchen. Her first inkling he was there came when he leaned down and kissed their son's baby-round cheek. "Good morning, *agape mou*." He turned to her, his expression cooling several degrees. "Good morning, Eden."

He was still smarting from her sexual rejection, she could tell. There was an air about him that said he hadn't slept any better than she had either.

"Off to Kouros Industries already?" she asked, indicating his briefcase with a nod of her head.

It was barely seven.

"I have an early morning meeting."

"Did you remember that you promised to take your mother and Vincent out to lunch today before they leave?" The older couple planned to return to their home and then come back to the villa in time for a family Christmas.

"I am hardly likely to forget a lunch date we made yesterday."

"I didn't mean to imply that you would, but when you don't have something on your calendar, you've been known to remember it too late to be of any use." She said it softly, not wanting another slanging match this morning.

Neither she, nor her heart, were up to it.

He sighed, apparently accepting her explanation. "I will meet you at the restaurant at one."

"Okay."

He turned to leave and then stopped. "Speaking of engagements, my diary shows a dinner with you tomorrow night."

"Yes." Thinking about that dinner and the reason for it had been part of what kept her up the night before.

"We will have to do it another time."

"Why?"

"Something has come up."

"With Kassandra?"

"With my business," he said on another sigh. "Out of town colleagues will be here one evening only."

"That night." And she just knew who she could thank for arranging the timing on this one.

"Yes. That night. Surely you do not mind postponing the dinner. It is not as if we do not eat together several nights a week. I suppose this was supposed to be some sort of a date without Theo, but in our current situation that seems overkill, do you not think?"

Overkill? Probably so. And why should she mind? It was only the anniversary of the day they met, after all. He had contrived to make it special since the beginning, but he certainly would not remember that now.

"By all means, cancel the dinner."

"I did not say cancel, I said postpone."

She ignored his argument over semantics and went back to feeding their son. He was the one who said a date in their current situation was ludicrous.

Aristide stood there, smoldering in silence for several seconds.

He glared down at her and then swung out of the house, an angry panther deprived of its prey.

Aristide wasn't surprised to see his brother and sister-in-law with Vincent and Phillippa when he reached the restaurant, but he was surprised Eden was not present at the table.

"Where is Eden?" he asked after greeting his mother and sister-in-law with a kiss.

"I do not know. We have not seen Eden all morning. We have been Christmas shopping," his mother replied.

"She called and said she was running late." Rachel

looked at Aristide as if wondering why his wife had chosen to call her instead of her own husband.

He had no answer for her, except that Eden no doubt planned to take avoiding him to new levels now that he'd cancelled their dinner date. His suspicion was confirmed when only minutes later his cell phone rang and it was Eden. She wasn't coming to lunch because Theo had just laid down for his afternoon nap and by the time she arrived it would be too late to eat with them.

She asked to speak to his mother and he passed the phone over, feeling gritty disappointment that he would not see his wife.

"Does she cancel like this often?" he asked after his mother flipped shut his mobile phone.

"Not at all, though I'm not surprised. If Theo needed her, she would not leave him. Eden has always been an exemplary mother and wife," his mother said with heavy-handed intimation.

"Has she?" he asked with bitter irony.

"What are you implying?" Sebastian demanded.

"If she was so wonderful, why did I forget her?"

Sebastian shook his head, clearly shocked by the question. "You were in a car accident…you had a concussion. That is excuse enough."

"Is it?"

"Oh, my heavens…you haven't voiced these suspicions to Eden, have you? That would devastate her," Rachel said, sounding worried.

Aristide thought silence the best defense at the moment.

His mother gave him a shrewd look and then shook her head. "You fool."

The condemnation was so aggravating, coming from

his doting mother, that he turned on her. "You are the one who told me my marriage was not all it should be."

"But I never said it was Eden's fault."

"You thought it was mine?" he asked in total shock.

"Well…yes. I thought you took your wife for granted, that you were naïvely certain her feelings for you would never change despite your neglect."

"I neglected her?" he demanded, one of his infernal headaches starting.

"Well, perhaps neglect is too strong a word, but you lived apart quite a bit. *By your choice*," she emphasized.

"Did you ever think that was because she was hard to live with?"

His entire family stared at him as if he'd lost his mind. Maybe he had. Maybe that is what losing one's memories did to one.

"Are you serious?" Sebastian demanded. "The only sweeter woman on the face of this earth than your wife is mine. Eden loves you so much, I almost pity her at times."

"Why the hell would you pity my wife?" Aristide asked in a near roar.

"Because she so obviously wanted to be with you and you seemed totally oblivious to how much your absences hurt her."

"Did you ever tell me this?"

"I tried." If looks could shrink a man, Sebastian's gaze would have turned Aristide into a Lilliputian. "You would not listen."

His mother was shaking her head at Aristide. "You are an idiot, my son. I am sorry to say it, but it is true. I thought you were smarter than your brother when you never doubted the parentage of your baby and married Eden right away." Sebastian grunted at this. "But I must say you are making up for that small act of wisdom with colossal stupidity now."

Lunch went downhill from there and by the time he got back to his office, Aristide felt attacked from all sides and his head hurt like someone was squeezing it in a vise.

Eden wandered down the hall of the spacious villa, feeling lost and disoriented. She was completely alone for the first time since discovering Aristide had forgotten her.

Phillippa and Vincent had left that afternoon and, because she and Aristide had planned to eat out tonight, the staff had the evening off. Theo was over at his Uncle Sebastian and Aunt Rachel's. When Eden had called to cancel their plans, Rachel had asked to have the baby anyway.

Her children had been looking forward to playing with their little cousin all week and were not at an age that they understood the changes wrought by their uncle's amnesia. Heck, she was a grown-up and she was struggling with comprehension.

She'd been clinging to her son since coming out of the hospital, needing the connection when everything had gone so terribly wrong with his father. Only it wasn't fair to the baby to keep him with her when he could be with his cousins having fun, so she'd let him go.

Without really understanding why she did it, she drifted into Aristide's room. There was nothing for her here. Just a tastefully decorated, tidy room that now housed her husband when once he had shared the master suite with her. The room's immaculate condition did not surprise her, but the sense of desolation that swept over her when she stopped beside the bed he now slept in did.

Emotions she had been holding in check since the accident fought to break free of the restraints she'd placed on them.

She shook her head against them, dropping to her knees beside the bed. His scent was there, on the carefully smoothed duvet, and she moaned as an ache that was both physical and soul-bruising slammed into her.

She'd tried to avoid physical proximity since his return from New York and moving into another bedroom. She refused to humiliate herself by letting him see how much she craved the comfort of his body. And she was afraid that if she let herself get too close, she would whimper like a pathetic, lost puppy, seeking her master's touch.

He still desired her. His telling her he wanted her had been proof of that, but climb down that it was from his position of separate beds, it had been hardly flattering.

So, he wanted to have sex with her. *That didn't mean anything.*

He still put Kassandra's feelings ahead of Eden's. Even if he didn't remember her, he knew she was his wife and she should be his first priority. A harsh bark of laughter erupted from her throat. What a joke that was.

Even when he'd remembered her, he hadn't put her first. She'd been a sexual convenience when they were dating, one he picked up and put down depending on his traveling schedule. At the time, she'd thought they had something special... just because he made an effort to spend time with her outside of bed. What a sap she'd been.

Their marriage had elevated her status in the eyes of others, but not his...she saw that now. Could not help seeing it. Even as the mother of his son, she'd only carried so much pull.

A whisper in the back of her mind tried to say it hadn't

been that bad, but the pain roaring through her drowned it out.

She hit the bed with her fist, wishing it was him. His willingness to cancel their dinner in favor of sharing one with his assistant was the final straw. Okay...so he didn't know that it was a special night, but he did know he'd made a commitment to spend it with her and he'd broken that commitment.

Eden hit the bed again and then collapsed on the floor in a fetal ball. She was worse than a forgotten wife; she was the despised wife—unimportant to Aristide in any way. He didn't even need her physically, not like she needed him. He might want her, but he was surviving celibacy just fine.

He didn't lay in bed night after empty night, longing for her presence, wishing for warmth that was never there.

Misery clenched her insides as tears burned her eyes. She couldn't fight it anymore and she stopped trying to. For once, it wasn't necessary. Everyone was gone and she was alone. She could cry out her grief without scaring her baby or having to explain herself to anyone.

She'd put on the brave front for Aristide's family, not wanting them to know how much his daily indifference hurt her. Not only for the sake of her pride, but for the sake of how they saw him. She'd even glossed over her emotional turmoil to her father when he called, wanting to know how she was doing now that she was back in Greece.

She refused to hurt her family by marriage and didn't trust her own father to understand or really care, so she'd carried the burden of grief alone. But it was too heavy and something inside her snapped under its weight.

She could hear her own racking sobs, but it was as if they were coming from someone else. She beat her fists against the floor over and over again until the sides of her hands were numb. It wasn't fair. She loved him. He didn't love her. She knew it. Wasn't that bad enough?

Why did she have to deal with the pain of being forgotten on top of it? Why? Her chest hurt from the violence of her tears and she didn't care. She lurched up and back on her heels screaming out, "Why? Why? *Why?*" between wrenching sobs.

She fell forward again, but something stopped her.

"Eden!" Aristide's hands were on her shoulders, their grip tight. "What is the matter?"

She shook her head and tried to pull away from him, unable to stand his touch. He wouldn't let go and she found herself pulled into his lap right there on the floor, his strong fingers pressing her face up so he could look in her eyes. "You must calm down, this kind of crying will make you sick."

"I—I…c-can't stop," she forced out between sobs.

"Yes, you can, baby. Hush," he soothed.

But she would not be comforted…he had called her baby again, a reminder she was not his wife…not really…not anymore. And that hurt so much, she would have doubled over with the pain of it if he had not been holding her so securely. An anguish-filled moan snaked out of her throat and her weeping increased.

He swore and started rubbing her back, talking to her in a gentle tone that barely penetrated her agonized mind. Eventually, however, a startling reality did manage to pierce her out-of-control grief—*Aristide was here with her, not at the dinner with Kassandra*. With a monumental effort, she forced herself to swallow back her sobs.

Hugging herself, she tried to keep her body from shuddering with more tears. "Y-you c-came h-home."

"I wanted to see Theo before he went to bed. Dinner is at seven-thirty." Aristide ruefully looked down at the tear splotches on his silk necktie. "It's a good thing I was already planning to change my suit."

The hope drained out of her. He had not come home for her…not even to see her before leaving again. He'd come for the baby. "He's not here," she said dully, too drained to even try to get off of his lap.

Aristide frowned, as if her tone bothered him. "Where is he?"

"At your brother's. It was already arranged and I didn't want to disappoint Rachel's children."

He nodded as if he understood that. "The staff are all gone too."

"They had the night off."

"Because of our dinner plans?"

"Yes."

His blue eyes filled with sensual speculation. "Presumably orchestrated so we would have privacy upon our return."

She just stared at him.

"Is that why you were crying? Because I had rescheduled our dinner?" he asked, sounding like he couldn't believe such a trivial matter could elicit her grief-stricken response.

"It doesn't matter."

It was his turn to simply look at her, his gentian blue gaze locked with hers for an eternity of seconds. "It will be all right, Eden."

She shook her head, the tears starting again, no matter how much she wanted to hold them back. "It won't be all right, not ever again. How can it be?"

He had married her for the sake of their unborn child—

now, would she stay married to him for the sake of both Theo and the unborn child he had forgotten even existed? No joy there. No hope of a future happiness, just years stretching ahead loving a man who didn't even remember making her his wife.

"You have to trust me."

"Trust you?" she asked, the concept unbelievable in her current circumstances. "You're just like my dad. I didn't see it at first, but that's because I was blinded by my own love for you." She gave a brittle laugh. "Like mother, like daughter."

"What do you mean?"

"Dad hurt my mom because he didn't really care about her either. Oh, he took care of her when she had cancer...much like you make sure I have everything I need, I suppose. And he acted grief-stricken when she died, but if he had really loved her, he couldn't have continued having affairs like he did."

"I am not having an affair," Aristide ground out.

"But you will keep hurting me until there isn't anything left."

"You have drawn this conclusion because I rescheduled one dinner date?" he asked with disbelief.

"I came to this conclusion because it is our reality!" She hated that he couldn't remember, that he looked at her now with incredulity. "I made a really big mistake getting involved with you to begin with, but I compounded it by marrying you."

And there was no way out...but how *could* she stay married to a man programmed to hurt her because he could not love her?

She started crying again, collapsing against his chest from a pain too intense to be borne. He did not try to calm her down this time, but silently held her, as if he under-stood this awful pain inside of her and her need to get it out. He couldn't possibly, but knowing that didn't seem to matter. His arms were a strong haven in a world she had stopped being able to tolerate and she desperately needed him to hold her.

She wept until there were no tears left and her throat was raw from her hoarse sobs. Even after she quieted, he held her. His silence helped her calm down better than any empty words could have done. She didn't know how long her crying jag had lasted, but she felt utterly drained of emotion.

Eventually, she stirred. "I've soaked your shirt." She spoke against his chest, unwilling to look into his face.

"As I said, I planned to change." He sounded curiously subdued.

Perhaps having a hysterical wife that he couldn't re-member crying all over him was too much for even Aris-tide's strong constitution.

Feeling uncomfortable in his embrace now that she had calmed down, she went to move off of his lap. "I guess you'd better get to it then."

"Not yet." His arms tightened around her so she could not move. "Tell me why you were crying."

She couldn't believe he couldn't understand. "Is it just you, or are all tycoons this dense when it comes to emo-tions?"

"I am not *dense*."

"As a London fog…oh, yes, you are."

"Why do you say that?"

"You asked me why I was crying." She sighed and let herself rest against him, too spent to fight or hide her peace at the contact.

He would push her away all too soon and she could go back to being a pregnant island in the hurricane of her life.

"And for this you believe I am stupid?"

"Yes."

He laughed harshly, the sound reverberating through her pliant body. "Were you always this unimpressed with me?"

"That's why I was crying."

"Because you think I am stupid and you are worried about the impact that will have on our son?" he teased, though his body was too tense for the words to come off as lighthearted as he obviously intended.

"Because you don't know how I felt before…because you forgot me. It was the final straw in a marriage that should never have happened to begin with."

The words hung between them for several seconds in utter silence. She could hear her heart beating, or was that his?

CHAPTER NINE

"I AM SORRY."

"Why? You're convinced I deserved it."

"No, I am not."

She wasn't buying it. He just didn't want her to start crying again. "Look, you'd better let me up. You've got things to do and so do I."

"What do you have to do?"

"Go dry off."

He laughed again; this time the sound was a little more natural. "I think we could both use a towel."

"Like you said, it's a good thing you planned on changing anyway. And speaking of…" she said, reminding him of his dinner engagement.

"You are making a habit of trying to send me away," he teased, making obvious reference to that morning as well.

Incapable of sharing his humor, she said sadly, "Usually, you are content to go."

He sighed as if acknowledging her mood. "Why did you not join Sebastian and Rachel this evening?"

"You're so sure they invited me?"

"Yes."

"That's quite an admission."

"What do you mean?"

"Well, that would imply that they like me a whole lot more than you do…which might mean you were wrong in your assessment of my character, wouldn't you say?"

"I have not said I do not like you…merely that I do not know you and am wary of our reasons for marrying."

He was slick at wiggling out of a tight spot, but she just shrugged. "If you say so."

"You did not answer my initial question."

And he wasn't going to let up until she did. "I didn't go with Theo to their house because I didn't feel like being around company tonight, all right?"

"You preferred to stay home and cry a river?"

"Something like that." She hadn't planned on the tears, but after all she'd been through recently, they were pretty much inevitable.

"I do not like seeing you cry." He sounded disgruntled by the admission.

"Don't let it worry you. It doesn't mean I'm anything special to you. You don't like seeing *any* woman cry."

"You are my wife. That is pretty special."

"You married me because I was pregnant with your son. That doesn't make me special, it only means I'm fertile."

"How can you make me laugh when my brain is telling me tragedy surrounds you like a shield?"

She shrugged. "Call it a gift."

He rubbed the top of her head with his chin, his arms wrapped tightly around her as if he could protect her from her pain. "I can't leave you like this."

"Sure you can."

"Do not tell me I have done so before."

"I'm not much of a cry baby."

"Which neatly sidesteps my question."

"I wasn't aware you asked a question. You made a statement. I didn't rebut it. You should be feeling vindicated in making it."

"Then why do I not?"

"I don't know."

"My family raked me over the coals at lunch today."

"Why?"

"Taking you for granted."

"They don't understand our marriage." And why she was making excuses for him when she agreed with his family, she didn't know.

He just sounded so bewildered by his family's censure. He wasn't used to it, that was for sure. She was pretty surprised herself. She'd never witnessed Sebastian, much less Phillippa, taking Aristide to task for anything.

"What is different about our marriage and that of my brother and his wife?"

"They love each other."

"And we do not?"

"I already told you that you don't love me."

"I told you this?"

"Not in so many words."

"I want you to stop being sad."

"I don't know if I can."

"Why?"

"Rejection isn't an easy thing to overcome. You, never having been the recipient of it, don't know that, but to put it delicately…it sucks."

He laughed again, the sound not exactly one of humor. "Are you saying I rejected you?"

"You forgot me. Isn't that the same thing?"

"No. As Sebastian reminded me today, I suffered a concussion…looking further for the cause of my amnesia is foolish."

"You don't want to sleep with me anymore."

"That is not true. I told you last night."

"But you don't need *me*."

"I do."

He meant physically, but her battered heart would take comfort where it could.

"You don't stay awake at night aching—" She cut herself off, but not before she had revealed more than she wanted to.

"Do you?"

"If I say yes, will your Greek pride be satisfied?"

"If I tell you that you are wrong, that you are not the only one who aches with a need that is not wholly physical, will your feminine pride be gratified?"

Not wholly physical? Did he mean it? "Are you saying that?"

"Yes, I am. And you?"

"Yes."

He tipped her chin up and pressed a soft, claiming kiss to her lips. "If I cancelled my dinner…if I stayed home and made love to my wife tonight, would you like that? Would you allow it?"

"Your dinner is too important…"

He pressed his finger against her lips. "No, Eden, it is not. I do not pretend to understand why our dinner date meant so much to you, but I hurt you when I broke it and I am sorry."

"It's the anniversary of the night we met."

Aristide heard the words without them registering at first. Kassandra had said she thought the dinner date with Eden was no big deal. He had believed her, trusting his long-time friend and personal assistant to know.

"You always contrived to make it a very special evening and canceling just reminded me how much we have lost." She made it sound like they were on the brink of divorce.

He wasn't going there. "You are still my wife."

But even if he was as dense in the emotional department as she had accused him of being, he was in tune with her enough to realize she wasn't looking at their marriage as an uncontested permanent part of her life.

He kissed her again, this time with all the hunger in his predator's soul. He could taste her tears and that did something to him, twisting his insides with unfamiliar pain. This woman was his wife and she was wrong about what that meant. *It did make her special*.

He kissed her until they were both breathing heavily, until she moaned with need and he ached with it.

He stood up with her in his arms and then carried her into their bedroom.

He laid her down in the center of their bed. "This is where we both belong."

She said nothing.

"I will not be leaving it again and neither will you."

"Are you sure about that?"

"Absolutely sure."

"Okay, then." She arched her back, the invitation to touch unmistakable.

He groaned, his sex so hard already, he thought he might explode before he got his clothes off. He tore out of his suit, ripping his soggy tie and shirt off with more impatience than finesse.

"You're certainly in a hurry," she said softly, the feminine laughter in her voice seducing his senses.

"I do not want you to change your mind." He said it jokingly, but part of him was very serious.

When she had turned him down the night before, he had felt a desperation he had not understood and liked even less.

She shook her head from side to side, her hair spreading out around her head like a silky brown halo. "Not a chance."

"That is good to know."

She smiled, Eve bent on seduction. "Take off your pants." The look in her eyes said this wasn't the first time she'd made such an order and he knew, from the response of his body, he'd liked it when she'd done so before.

She was not an aggressive woman, so for her to make sexual demands would be the most erotic form of lovemaking.

He stepped out of his shoes, before toeing off his socks. Then peeling his slacks away, he pushed his boxers down with them. He stood completely naked before her, his body throbbing with the need to join with hers.

She stared at him, her chest rising and falling with shallow pants. Her pretty gray eyes were so dark with passion they were almost black as her gaze moved over him like a hot caress. "You are so beautiful, Aristide."

He felt a twinge in the region of his heart. No other woman had ever called him that. Sexy, yes. Masculine. Buff, even, but never beautiful. He liked it, though he would never admit it out loud.

She kicked her shoes off, but when she went to pull her shirt off, he shook his head. "Stop."

Stilling, her eyes wide, she asked, "Why?"

"I want to unwrap you like a present."

She swallowed and hope flared in her eyes, making them shine with silver lights. "You used to say that to me all the time."

He didn't want to think about before, the time he couldn't remember. He only wanted to think about now. In a rush that made her gasp, he came down over her. His entire being jolted with pleasure as they made contact. The layer of her clothes could have been gone for all the notice his body took of the barrier.

"Aristide...what is it?" she asked, her voice catching as he settled himself between her legs and rubbed the apex of her thighs with his iron-hard sex.

"No more talking," he growled and then devoured her lips with his own, his kiss primal and hungry, demanding a response.

When she opened her lips on a small moan, he swept inside, claiming the warm wetness as his. He could not remember making this woman his own, but tonight she would know without doubt she belonged to him in the most primitive and binding way a woman could belong to a man.

She locked her legs behind his hips and arched into him.

He shuddered with pleasure and could not help pressing down, increasing the friction—though it undermined his control.

She felt so small beneath him and yet so womanly, more tantalizing than any woman had ever been. Her tiny curves drove him to madness and he cupped her breast, glorying when her nipple peaked instantly. He did not have to remember to get her to react to his touch...to be a husband in every sense of the word.

He played with the rigid bud through her top, realizing immediately that she was not wearing a bra. The knowledge made him desperate to touch the bare skin he knew waited for him under the cotton of her snug-fitting T-shirt.

Aristide's hand slipped under the hem of her top and

glided up her ribcage, the light touch of his fingertips against her skin giving Eden chills. He stopped below the curve of her breast, his thumb brushing back and forth in a teasing caress that made her whimper into his mouth with need.

She ached for him to touch her breasts the way he'd touched them so many times before.

But would it be like it had been before? Or would it be different because she was a stranger to him?

It didn't matter. She remembered him and wanted him. She needed this confirmation of her importance to him. His hand made contact with her breast and her thoughts exploded in a maelstrom of feeling. The caress was familiar and yet it wasn't. It had a tentative quality that hadn't been there since the first time they made love, as if he was trying to figure out what pleased her.

She could have told him it didn't matter. He had never touched her in a way that did not wring pleasure from her. But she was too busy kissing him to say anything, not to mention too busy reveling in the deep concentration he gave to the task.

He played with her breasts, squeezing them and then teasing their rigid peaks with knowing fingers. He didn't know she was pregnant and yet he instinctively did not press too hard on her ultra-sensitive skin. He was good at this, an expert.

She started to moan and thrash under him, finally tearing her mouth from his to beg for more.

But it was still several minutes of teasing foreplay before he began unwrapping her like a present as promised. Would he notice she was pregnant? She barely showed a difference in her waistline and he didn't remember what she'd looked like before, but the thought was tantalizing.

To have all the secrets revealed, to be able to share her pregnancy with her husband.

He touched her in a way that sent all thoughts in her head exploding into space. He kissed every inch of skin he exposed, starting with her feet and then paying close attention to her already highly stimulated curves. He laved the turgid peaks like an ice-cream cone and she shivered with delight.

He growled against her skin, the sound so animal-like she shivered again…this time an atavistic fear mixed with her sensual pleasure.

He had left her panties on and slid his hand inside as if he knew she found this pseudo-secret touch highly erotic.

Maybe he did. Maybe part of him was trying to remember. Her insides melted at the thought. Wanting desperately for it to be the way it had been before, she responded to him with all the trust and joy she had ever given him and prayed that this time of intimacy would restore their marriage in more ways than one.

It wasn't hard to pretend she was as important to him as she needed to be, not when for the first time in their married life, he'd opted out of his business dinner to stay home and make love with her.

Even as she had the thought, his cell phone started ringing.

He reared back, saying a harsh Greek word she knew but had never used herself. "Give me thirty seconds, all right, *pethi mou*? Then we will be left in peace."

She bit her lip, hoping the interruption did not mean the end of their time of intimacy.

He cupped her cheek. "Trust me."

"Okay."

He smiled and then dove for the ringing phone still attached to the waistband of his trousers.

Forcing back her fear that Kassandra would get to him yet again, she sat up and watched his big, gorgeous body move. It was no hardship considering the excellent view she had of his very fine backside. He had muscles *everywhere*.

He flipped the phone open and turned to face her at the same time.

Noticing where her gaze had been directed, he grinned with masculine confidence and said, "Aristide here," into the phone.

"Where are you?" Kassandra was so agitated, Eden could hear her through the phone.

He looked down at himself and then at Eden with a droll expression. "Something has come up and I will have to forgo the dinner tonight."

Eden choked on her laughter at the *double entendre* and bit her fist to stop the sound from escaping her lips.

Aristide climbed back on the bed and leaned over Eden. She fell back into the pillows, mesmerized by the hot promises bombarding her from his blue eyes.

"I am sure you can handle it. You are my personal assistant for a reason."

He rubbed himself against Eden and she had to bite back a moan of delight as Kassandra said something else.

He went rigid. "Perhaps you have forgotten who the employer is in this relationship, but I do not require advice from you on how to order my priorities."

Eden stopped in the act of reaching up to kiss his flat male nipple and her gaze flew to his. She could just imagine how Kassandra would respond to the reprimand. The woman was a master manipulator.

Aristide shook his head as if he could read Eden's mind.

His mouth thinned in a frown and his eyes narrowed in obvious displeasure. "We will have to discuss that Monday morning, Kassandra. Until then, I am unavailable."

He switched off the phone, flipped it shut and tossed it on to the floor and then turned back to face her. "I think it is time I finished unwrapping my present."

Euphoria filled her. He'd dismissed his personal assistant for her. Not only that, he had turned off his phone. The last time he had done that she had been in labor with Theo.

Most importantly, *Aristide had stayed for her.*

Happy tears burned her eyes and she smiled. "I'd like that."

His brow creased and he brushed at a single tear that had escaped. "Is something wrong?"

"No, it's just so right, I can barely stand it."

"Ah…so, these are tears of happiness."

She nodded, her voice too choked to speak.

"I am glad." He slid down her body, his mouth wreaking havoc with her nervous system.

"Oh, Aristide…it's so perfect with you."

"It is you who are perfect. Perfectly shaped." He kissed each of her turgid peaks, nipping them and she gasped. "Perfectly responsive." He pressed his lips to each of her ribs and then slid his mouth along her hot skin to explore her belly button with his tongue. "Perfectly lovely. Ah…my Eden."

It wasn't *yineka mou*, but it was close, and she felt sure his memories were only a breath away as she arched helplessly against him.

When he used his teeth to effect the final unveiling, pulling her panties down her legs with sexy mastery, she just about fainted from the pleasure of it. And he wasn't even touching her most private flesh yet…

Then he spread her legs and kissed her with an intimacy she could only ever imagine sharing with this man.

She cried out as his tongue brought her to almost immediate fulfillment, her insides clenching with cataclysmic pleasure. He didn't stop, but kept pleasuring her until the ecstasy of his touch left her wrung out and limp.

Only then did he move up her body to press himself against the throbbing entrance to her feminine core. His eyes asked a question and she grabbed his hips, pulling him to complete his possession. It was a ritual as old as the very first time they made love…he always asked in some way for permission to enter her body and waited for her acquiescence.

Sometimes she used that wait to tease him until she thought he might take her without it, but he never did. He had more self-control than anyone she had ever known.

As he eased inside of her, she felt closer to him than she had in months and couldn't help crying out, *"I love you, Aristide."*

His mouth slammed down on hers as if taking possession of the words, the kiss so intense that she lost herself in it. He made love to her with driving passion until they came together in a hurricane of ecstasy.

Afterward, he rolled on to his back, keeping their bodies connected like he had so many times before. She settled her head against his chest, listening to his heartbeat and letting the precious intimacy soak into her every pore.

He took a deep breath and let it out. "That was amazing."

She couldn't help grinning against his chest. "Worth skipping your business dinner?"

"Definitely. And you…did it make this night special enough for you?"

"I would say that finding each other again is a very fitting way to celebrate our first meeting."

His arms tightened around her. "Was it this good before?"

She pushed up on to her forearms, tilting her head so they were eye to eye. "You don't remember?"

"No."

"But…"

"What?"

"You made love to me like you remembered. That wasn't the intimacy between strangers," she said helplessly.

He affected a small shrug under her as if it was of little importance. "Obviously, our bodies know each other."

Or he had made love to every woman before her like he did to her. She'd never considered the possibility before, having assumed that it was as special for him as it was for her. Her stomach churned with the possibility that what she took for tender intimacy was, in fact, well-developed technique.

"What is it? You are frowning."

"I thought if anything could jar your memory of me, it would be our lovemaking."

"Is that why you allowed me to touch you?" he asked, his voice no longer lazy and warm.

"No."

But something in her face must have given her away because he glared. "Tell me," he insisted.

"It was my plan when you came back from New York."

"So that was why you were upset I wanted to sleep in a separate bed. You hoped to bring back my memory with sex."

"That was part of it, yes."

If he'd gone rigid during his call with Kassandra, that was nothing compared to his reaction now. "And this…" He pressed her hips down with hard hands, deepening his entry in her body. "It was all just a test?"

"No." Horrified at his reaction, she shook her head vehemently. "We made love because we both needed to… didn't we?"

She'd told him she loved him. And like all the times she'd said the words before, he had not responded in kind. At the moment she'd said it, his lack of response had not bothered her, but now it stung like a thousand wasps attacking her heart.

He relaxed a little. "Yes, we both needed it."

But had he needed her, or only a body? She'd never stopped to consider how she would feel after making love to a man who did not know her. It wasn't good…even though they were married, even though she loved him, she felt shame because she couldn't be sure he'd been making love to her and not simply a body.

She pressed against his chest. "I need to get up now."

The last vestiges of his anger drained from his face and his eyes gleamed with sensual anticipation. "I am not finished."

"I am."

"Because I did not remember you?"

How could she answer that? "The simplistic answer is yes," she admitted, "but it's a lot more complicated than that."

"Explain it to me."

"Let me up."

Despite their near argument, he had never completely lost his arousal and now it was growing.

He tilted his pelvis up, sending shivers of sensation

through her. "No. You want me. Your body betrays just how much with every tiny movement."

She couldn't deny it. Her nipples were hard and aching for his attention all over again and her most secret flesh was clinging to him with pulsing strength.

She said the only thing she could say…the only thing he might understand. "But you don't want me."

"Wrong."

"You don't. Not *me*," she said earnestly. "I could be any woman to you."

"But you are not *any* woman. You are my wife."

"You don't know me," she cried, frustration and hurt filling her.

"How well did I know you the first time we made love?"

She stopped trying to get away, her face heating with an instant blush. "We made love the first time on our second date."

His smile was triumphant. "Then I could not have known you any better then than I do now."

His logic left her speechless for several seconds. "It is not the same," she finally responded lamely.

"How is it different?"

"You wanted to know me then. You pursued me."

"Not very hard, if it was only our second date."

"I was an easy mark for you."

"You were and are the woman I want." He proved it by surging up into her, fully aroused and ready to make love again.

She averted her face. "I never intended to make love with a man who was not my husband."

"And yet you were my lover for over a year before we married."

"Yes," she whispered, the lingering disappointment in herself in her voice.

He tilted her chin toward her. "You knew that was the longest relationship I had ever had with a woman?"

"I wasn't even sure we had a relationship. You never introduced me to your family."

"I wanted to keep you to myself."

"How do you know?" she asked deridingly. "You don't remember."

"But as I have told you, I know myself. I know what would have motivated me in the situation you describe."

"I believed it was because I was not important to you."

"The fact you are now my wife proves that was not the case."

She refused to remind him again that he had married her for the sake of their unborn son. He seemed to forget it and she only wished she could.

Despite the physical response of her body to their continued intimacy, she felt numb inside as she realized the one hope she had to reclaim her marriage was gone.

"We have talked enough."

"Yes, I suppose we have."

Ignoring her melancholy, he began the seduction all over again. She had no defense against him and didn't want any. At least if they made love she would not feel this awful inner frozenness that seemed to be spreading from her heart outward.

CHAPTER TEN

EDEN was sitting on the floor, her back to him and playing with Theo the next afternoon when Aristide walked into the large living room. She'd pulled her silky brown hair up into a casual ponytail that revealed the delicate column of her neck. The snug-fitting cotton top and jeans she wore only served to remind him of the night before and how much pleasure he had found in her delicious body.

His own tightened with need at the memory.

But, damn it, it had been more than a slaking of lust…she'd been right. They had not made love like strangers, so why did he feel more like one with her today than he had before returning to her bed?

"So you are back from shopping," he said.

She'd left that morning, refusing his offer to accompany her on the pretext she needed to buy his Christmas gift.

"Yes," she replied without turning.

"You have been home long?"

"Not really." Long enough to change her clothes and collect their son from the nursery.

She had not sought out Aristide upon her return, but there was no surprise there. She'd been like this since they got up that morning—even more distant from him than she had been since his return from New York. It was as if she had completely cut herself off emotionally from him and after their lovemaking, that was not an attitude he could live with.

"I have made dinner reservations for tonight." He had called the restaurant, figuring she must like the place if they had planned to eat there originally.

It had been a long time since he had done something so mundane, but he doubted she would appreciate that fact.

She looked over her shoulder at him and smiled vacantly, then turned back their son, her smile for Theo much more natural. She tickled his tummy, talking in baby talk to him.

"Did you hear me?"

She stiffened, but then seemed to force herself to relax. "Yes, but it's not necessary. As you said the other day, we hardly have a normal relationship. A date would be superfluous."

"I do not agree."

She shrugged and he saw red. She hadn't even spoken and he was ready to blow his top. No woman got to him like this…hell, no person got to him like this.

He took a firm grip on his unreasonable temper. "I think we need to get to know each other."

"I already know you."

"Then I need to get to know you," he said from between gritted teeth. When she did not respond, he said, "We must accept that my memory may never come back and plan accordingly."

Her body jerked in reaction to his words, but that was the only response he got.

"I know it must hurt you to hear I may never remember you," he said, feeling more hesitant than he ever had, "but it has to be acknowledged."

Gurgled laughter erupted from his son's throat, startling Aristide. The baby had grabbed one of his toys scattered on the floor and begun playing with it. It was a jack-in-the-box and Theo had mastered turning the handle until the clown popped out. The childish music filled the silence that felt like an oppressive weight around them.

Finally, Eden turned to face Aristide, her expression stoic. "So you want to get to know me and decide if I'm worthy of being your wife."

"I did not say that."

"Then, what is the purpose?"

"Is it so hard for you to understand me wishing to get to know my wife?"

"We don't need to go out on dates for you to do that. You can do so just as well here…when you are home."

"I want to take you out," he ground out, annoyed by the reminder of his many absences.

He intended to change that, but didn't make the mistake of telling her so. She was in no mood to take anything he said at face value.

She sighed. "You don't have to court me all over again. I'm already your wife."

"It does not sound like there was much of a courtship the first time around."

She flinched and he cursed his quick tongue.

"Whatever you call our relationship before, it's done and we're married. To coin one of your own phrases, dating now would be nonproductive."

"I do not agree."

She rolled her eyes. "Why is it such a big deal to you?"

"Why are you fighting it so hard?"

"Maybe I've finally decided to accept the status quo of our marriage."

For some reason, that sent a cold chill up his spine. "And maybe *I have not*."

"Why not?" she asked, the ice finally cracking to give him a glimpse of the hurting woman beneath the brittle façade. "You've got everything a man like you wants out of marriage. A faithful wife who will provide you with children and warm your bed when you want it. It's all you ever wanted from me and I've finally accepted that, all right?"

Her voice was choked with tears, but she didn't let them fall. "You can keep right on working your terrible hours, traveling half the time and spending more after-office hours with your personal assistant than your wife."

He didn't know how to rebut her words without memories to back up his claims, so he said the one thing she could not deny. "As of Monday morning, I will no longer have a personal assistant."

Eden went paper-white and swayed.

He dropped to his knee beside her and grabbed her shoulders. "Are you all right?"

"Did you just say that Kassandra quit?" she asked in a frail and disbelieving voice.

"No."

Her eyes closed as if in pain. "I didn't think it could be—"

"I plan to fire her," he said before she could go on.

Eden's eyes flew open and she stared at him with a hope that hurt him to see. "Say that again."

"I will be firing Kassandra the first thing Monday morning."

"But you can't," she whispered, her voice thready.

LUCY MONROE   147

Her reaction categorically told him his decision had
been the right one. "I assure you, I can."

"But why would you?"

"She told me that last night was nothing more than a
regular dinner date that you would not mind canceling."

"She was wrong, but I hardly see how that would lead
you to fire her."

"As my personal assistant, there is no way she could be
unaware of such a significant date. When I realized this, I
had to ask myself what other lies she had told me about
you. The more I thought about it, the more I realized there
have been many. Since she seems to be the only person
who believes you are anything like Andrea Demakis, it fol-
lows she lied about that as well."

He did not know why he had forgotten his lovely wife,
but if she was the wife from Hades, he was Santa Claus.

Eden swallowed, blinking back more tears. "She was
trying to destroy our marriage."

He could not doubt her view of events. Nothing else
made sense in the circumstances. "For a long time?" he
asked.

"Since the beginning."

"Why?"

"She wants you."

"I do not want her."

Eden looked unconvinced.

He could not fault her for that. He had taken Kassandra's part on more than one occasion since he woke from
his coma. He did not know how to explain to Eden the vulnerability he had felt in a world where everyone around
him knew a piece of the puzzle that remained a mystery
to him...his wife. He had relied on a woman he thought
he knew and could trust.

"I am sorry I let her influence me and hurt you."

"You believed she was your friend."

"Only she wanted more than friendship."

"According to her, you had it."

"Once…we had a very short affair about three years ago."

"Right around when we met."

"I broke it off. If it was before or after we met, I do not know, but I do know that I would not sleep with two women at the same time."

His wife nodded, though doubt still haunted her soft gray eyes. "I'll talk to Rachel about leaving Theo with her for our date."

Relief that was out of proportion to her acceptance surged through him. "Surely we have someone who can watch him here."

"I prefer family and so does Rachel…it's worked out well for us in the past."

"You are saying you rarely leave Theo." He smiled, thoroughly approving.

"That's not what I was saying, but it is true."

"Sebastian told me that the trip to New York was the first one you accompanied me on. Was that your decision, or mine?"

"Yours."

His jaw clenched. That is what he had thought from everything that had been said, but he had to be sure. "I see. And you did not mind?"

She turned her head away. "I would rather not answer that."

"Why not?" Damn it, there was so much he did not know.

"It may not have occurred to you, but there is a lot of humiliation for me in our current situation."

"Why should you be humiliated?"

"You're brilliant…everyone says so. You figure it out."

Just then Theo demanded her attention by grabbing her shirt and lifting himself to stand in front of her.

She turned back to their baby. "You're going to be walking soon, aren't you?" she asked with a smile and her heart full of love for her beautiful son.

Frustrated by the interruption, but glad for the progress that had been made, Aristide said, "If he does, heaven help us."

She laughed, the sound not quite natural. "He is one energetic little bundle."

Remembering what it had been like at his brother's that morning when he had gone to pick up Theo, he said, "I cannot imagine having two like Sebastian and Rachel do. Not yet, anyway."

She went all stiff again. "You always said you wanted a half-dozen children."

"Spaced appropriately apart, it is my fondest wish."

Eden put her earrings on with trembling fingers. It took three tries to get the diamond teardrops in place. She was going on a date with her husband and more nervous than a teenager going to her first prom.

He was going to fire Kassandra.

She couldn't take it in. When Eden had criticized his P.A. in New York before he lost his memory, he had staunchly stood up for the other woman. Now, without any prompting from Eden, he was suddenly willing to give Kassandra the heave-ho…all because she had lied and Aristide realized it.

He had no memory of the importance of their anniversary dinner date, but he'd reasoned that Kassandra would.

Eden smiled. He really did have a brilliant brain, even if he couldn't figure out why it would bother her to expose the depth of her feeling in contrast to his.

She wished she knew if he was getting rid of the other woman because she had hurt Eden, or because a liar could not be trusted. Eden hoped it was at least a little bit of the former.

Regardless, the wicked witch was being banished and Aristide showed every evidence of truly wanting to make their marriage work. Eden had not been able to accomplish so much in over a year of marriage.

She felt like dancing around the room in celebration.

Okay, so there was a strong possibility that Kassandra would talk her way out of being fired. The woman was a master at circumventing Aristide's good intentions, but Eden didn't want to dwell on that unpleasant possibility. Her husband was too smart to go on being taken in by his personal assistant, no matter how good a liar she was.

Eden went back to her preparations, but a sudden thought froze her in the act of applying a light coat of mascara. If he remembered her and their past together, would he go back to being the way he'd been before the accident? Would their marriage once again take a backseat to his business?

She would rather she remained the forgotten wife than have that happen.

Aristide took her to their favorite restaurant and regardless of how he had discovered which one it was, she appreciated the effort.

She smiled at him as they were seated at their usual table. "Thank you for bringing me here."

"Does it have special memories?" For once the reminder of his selective amnesia did not hurt.

"Yes. The man who owns it has a brother who migrated to New York. We ate at his restaurant on our first date and many times after. You brought me here the first time to celebrate seeing our baby through ultrasound. When you told me the relationship to the other restaurant, I cried like an idiot."

His sexy blue gaze melted her. "I bet I loved it."

She laughed. "As a matter of fact, you did. You hate unhappy tears, but seem to get a very perverse pleasure out of making me cry for sentimental reasons."

He reached across the table and took her hand. "Maybe I just like making you happy."

"Then why did you leave me behind when you traveled?" she asked in a voice laced with remembered hurt, then felt instant guilt.

No way could he know the answer to that one. If she didn't watch out, she was going to ruin the present with pain from the past.

But he didn't look upset by her question. His face wore its usual expression of casual self-assurance. "I do not know. When we were in New York, you said you did not think I was ready for marriage and perhaps you were right. However, I am content to be married now."

"Does that mean you won't travel so much?"

"I have no desire to be separated from you and Theo for long periods of time."

Which wasn't a direct answer, but was a whole lot more promising than his former attitude. Only, how could he be content to be married now when he had been so intent on maintaining emotional independence before? He barely knew her...so what was the difference? Had there been something about her that he had been unable to connect to on an intimate level before? More importantly, would he rediscover that something the more time they spent together now?

"Suddenly you look terrified, *yineka mou*. Tell me what is frightening you. I do not think it is the prospect of spending more time with me," he said with teasing confidence.

"You called me *your woman*."

"*My wife, my woman*…you are both of these things, are you not?"

"Yes, but you said before that I didn't feel that way to you. That you did not feel like a husband."

"We made love," he said as if that should explain it all—and maybe for him, it did.

Men could be so basic and, for all his sophistication, Aristide had a primitive streak in his character a mile wide.

His thumb brushed her palm and he smiled with predatory intent. "Do not think you will sidetrack me from my question. What had you looking so afraid?"

She bit her lip, thoroughly seduced by this man who had showed more interest in her emotional condition in two days than he had the entire time they had been lovers and then married. "What if you change?"

"Why should I?"

When she told him her reasoning, he frowned. "I know you a lot better than you think I do. Whatever prompted my behavior before, it was not a flaw in your character I am yet to find."

"How can you be sure?"

"Because I have spent every day since waking from my coma trying to find flaws in you that are not there. All I have found is a woman I was smart to make my own and then marry."

His wording was odd, but then she realized with his primal view of sex, he probably considered her his from the moment they became lovers.

"I will not change my mind about you."

She hoped he was right because her heart would shrivel up and die if their marriage went back to being what it had been. It was an incredible thought considering how much she had wanted that very thing only twenty-four hours ago, but the kind of relationship he seemed to be offering now was everything her dreams were made of.

But if he was right and there was a chance he wasn't going to regain his memory, shouldn't she tell him about the baby? She knew she couldn't. And secretly she didn't want to. She wanted to know this time that he was staying with her for her own sake. She needed that assurance.

Besides, this time she doubted he would be as delighted with her pregnancy as he had been the first time. She was fairly certain he would not consider a year and a half *proper spacing*.

On the other hand, could she hold him accountable for a throwaway remark made with no knowledge of his impending second time at fatherhood? He loved being a daddy and she doubted even his image of the perfectly spaced family could diminish his enthusiasm for the role a second time around.

She hoped.

Regardless, it was simply something she refused to bring into the equation of their marriage right now.

When the roses Aristide had ordered were delivered to their table, Eden gasped and then gaped when she saw the jeweler's box nestled in the center of the arrangement.

"Open it," he instructed.

Her hand trembled as she lifted the small black velvet box from the foliage and it was all he could do not to pull her around the table and into his arms. She was so damned vulnerable. Had he realized that before, or had she been better at hiding it?

She snapped the ring box open and gasped again, the sound almost a sob. "It's beautiful."

He had the anniversary ring delivered earlier that day while she'd been out shopping and then sent it to the florist to include in the bouquet.

He did not know what he had originally planned to give Eden to celebrate the anniversary of when they first met. He had searched through his diary to no avail. Kassandra probably knew, but he did not trust her to tell him the truth about it. More likely she would have encouraged him to get something that would cause Eden further pain or some level of embarrassment.

He did not know what caused a woman he had trusted as close as family to turn on his wife, but he was convinced Eden had not provoked it.

"Does it fit?" The jeweler had taken a guess based on the size of her ring finger.

She slipped the diamond anniversary band on and nodded, her lips quivering suspiciously.

"Do not start crying again."

"It comes with the territory right now."

He supposed she meant living through the trauma of being forgotten by her husband, but those were happy tears if he'd ever seen any.

She stretched her hand out to admire the ring, her rainwater eyes glistening. "It's really gorgeous."

"Not half as gorgeous as the woman wearing it, *yineka mou*."

Her gaze flew to his and something hit him straight in the gut. She had said he didn't need to court her again… that they were already married, but he realized he *wanted* to court her. He wanted her to feel good about being married to him, not stuck with a man who could not remember the first time they had met, much less made love.

His pride demanded it, but so did something powerful in the region of his heart.

Aristide pulled Eden into his arms to dance with a strong feeling of relief. He had wanted to hold her since looking across the table and seeing the vulnerable expression in her lovely gray eyes.

They had talked throughout dinner and she had shown a surprising understanding of business. She'd explained that she had worked for her father, an American business tycoon, before moving away from New York City to pursue her real loves…art and history. Apparently, she had been an assistant curator for a small museum in upstate New York when they met.

The job fit her and he wondered if she missed it, but when he asked her, she said she really loved full-time motherhood and her volunteer work with an Athens-based museum society fed her interest.

The more he learned of her, the more he realized his wife was a very special and precious woman.

Not to mention sexy. She felt so good against him—too good—and his body had a predictable response he made no effort to hide from her.

"We'd better stay out here a long time if you don't want to be embarrassed exiting the dance floor," she teased in a husky voice against his chest.

Instead of pulling away, as he'd half-expected from his rather shy wife, she snuggled up against him.

The feel of her soft stomach pressing against his hard flesh tormented him and increased his arousal tenfold. "We may not make it off the dance floor at all if you keep that up."

Her husky laughter sent jolts of pleasure zinging through him and it took all his self-control not to carry her off the dance floor and to some private spot to make love. This woman could seduce him with a look. Was the knowledge of that power what had made him hold himself apart from her?

It had certainly contributed to his wariness since the accident. It could very well be the source of the sense of foreboding he had had surrounding his marriage. Considering his family's past, it made sense that he would find it hard to trust a woman who could wield that kind of power over him.

However, he did not see keeping her at a distance the safe course of action now.

It was patently clear to him that he had been on the verge of losing her when he lost his memory…at the very least, their marriage had been in some real trouble. He'd handled a lot of things badly since coming out of his coma, but he could and would fix them.

Eden's body sang with desire as Aristide carried her into their bedroom and kicked the door shut. He turned to lock it, ensuring their privacy. He had insisted on carrying her from the car because he said he could not remember carrying her over the threshold and wanted that memory now.

How could she turn down such a romantic request, even if she wanted to? And she hadn't.

She had always loved being carried by him and if he could remember, he would know that he had made a habit of it.

But tonight it was even more special. He'd been the epitome of a romantic escort all evening—wining and dining her, and dancing with her in a way that was guaranteed to seduce her senses. There was no doubt he was intent on completing the seduction now and all she wanted to do was let him.

She still didn't quite trust him, but she loved this side to him and wanted to enjoy the benefits while it lasted. Heck, she loved him period and doubted that would ever change. She would grasp the moments of happiness as they came and worry about the future…well…in the future.

And if he really did get rid of Kassandra, maybe that future had a chance of being something truly wonderful.

Eden focused on the pleasure of her husband's mouth claiming hers.

He broke the kiss with a masculine groan of pleasure. "You taste so good, *agape mou*."

He licked her lips, teasing along the seam with the tip of his clever tongue and applying gentle pressure for her to open up. She let her lips part, inviting him inside with a small foray of advance and retreat. He took the invitation, sliding his tongue along hers, possessing the interior of her mouth with tender mastery.

She ran her hands over his shoulders and chest and face, everywhere she could touch, imprinting the warmth of his body on her senses. He felt and smelled so good… so masculine…so much her husband…her mate. Craving bare skin, she started undoing buttons so she could get her hand inside his shirt.

They both moaned when her hand came into contact with his hair-roughened chest. He was so strong, his muscles so hard they felt like velvet-covered steel under her hand. She found his nipple and circled it with her forefinger, over and over again, until it was hard. She pressed the small nub between her thumb and forefinger, that special spot between her legs growing moist and throbbing when he groaned into her mouth and tightened his hold on her almost bruisingly.

She needed to feel the entire expanse of his naked chest. She attacked his jacket, maneuvering it off, one arm at a time. It was hard to do without breaking their kiss, but she managed it, her legs swinging down and locking around his waist when he let them go so she could finish removing his jacket. The tie came off with relative ease, but his shirt had to be untucked from his slacks. She got it out, unbuttoning the last few buttons, and pushed the garment off his broad shoulders.

When she had him undressed from the waist up, she went back to exploring his torso, this time her questing fingers making his big body shudder as he moaned out his pleasure.

She wanted naked skin against naked skin, but couldn't stop touching him long enough to get her own clothes off.

Clearly he had the same idea because he started tugging her dress up with one hand while holding her against him with the other arm. He succeeded in getting her dress over her head, only breaking the kiss once and leaving her in nothing but her thigh-highs and panties.

She hadn't worn a bra and was grateful for that fact now as she pressed her swollen breasts against his hard chest.

His mouth broke from hers and he hissed as if the touch burned him. Heavens, it probably did…it felt like it was burning her. Her nipples stung where they were in contact with the dark curls covering his chest and she rubbed herself against him, increasing the friction and the pleasure.

"You are so sexy, Eden."

She was too busy kissing along his jaw and down his neck to answer. She found the place where his neck met his shoulder and sampled that favorite spot with her tongue, reveling in the salty maleness of his skin.

His hand slipped down her back, under the silk of her panties and cupped her bare bottom. He started kneading her flesh, his fingers coming perilously close to the apex of her thighs, but never quite touching the place that needed his touch most.

She softly nipped at his neck and ground her sweet spot against the hard ridge hidden by his trousers.

The world shifted and she found herself lying on their bed while he tore out of his slacks for the second time in twenty-four hours.

She pushed her panties off, but when she went to roll her thigh-highs down, he said, "No…leave them on."

His guttural demand sent a shiver down her spine and she leaned back on the bed, remembering how much he loved her in thigh-highs and nothing else.

Reaching her hands out toward him, she widened her legs in a double invitation.

He came down over her in a sensual rush and pressed inside of her with one smooth, darkly intense movement. *"You are mine."*

"Yes, and you are mine." She arched up against him, the sensation so incredible she could barely maintain conscious thought.

He drove into her with an animal-like growl and they made love with a raw intensity unlike any they had shared in all the passionate encounters of their relationship.

She felt the pleasure spiraling inside her, tightening, tightening, tightening…until it exploded. It radiated outward on a wave of such intense ecstasy, she could not bite back a primal scream of joy—despite the last bit of her sanity telling her that tonight they were not alone in the villa.

Aristide's roar was no more controlled as his body went rigid with his release.

Afterward, he collapsed on top of her, his breathing every bit as ragged as her own. "*S'gapo, yineka mou*. I love you."

Everything inside her clenched in rejection of the words. "No…you can't…"

CHAPTER ELEVEN

HE REARED back and looked down at her, his expression grim and almost frighteningly primitive. "I do."

"You didn't before. It's just the sex...it overwhelmed me too. I'm still overwhelmed," she admitted with a panting breath.

He shook his head as if trying to clear it. "You told me you loved me last night. Do not deny it."

Ah...that explained it. "I won't deny it. I do love you, but you don't have to feel obligated to return the words in kind. You never have before."

"I am saying it now."

"You don't have to. Honestly. Please, don't worry about it, Aristide. I know you don't love me, but I've learned to accept it."

He jumped off of her with an angry movement and then stood beside the bed, vibrating with outrage. "I did not say I love you because I thought you were expecting it."

Those stupid pregnancy-driven hormones were making her eyes water again and she tried to blink the tears away. "I didn't mean to offend you." She swallowed, her insides hollow at how the most amazing experience of her life was being ruined by words. Words she had always wanted to hear, but knew could not be true. "It's just…I don't want you telling me you love me out of some misplaced sense of guilt."

"Of what do I have to feel guilty over?"

"Nothing…I…" She shook her head, unable to go on.

"Do not cry," he growled.

"I won't." She turned her head and sniffed, blinking furiously.

He swore and the bed dipped beside her. Then she was in his arms, his body wrapped around hers. "I love you, but since I supposedly did not love you before, you find it impossible to believe now. Is that not true?"

Eden tilted her head back, her gray eyes filled with wary uncertainty and Aristide wanted to curse again.

"Well, if you were going to love me, wouldn't you have discovered it before this? I mean, you were really happy when Theo was born, so proud, I thought you would burst, but you didn't tell me you loved me then."

And she had been hoping he would, just as she had hoped the night before that making love would reclaim his memories of her. He ground his teeth in an effort not to say anything damaging. His lack of memory was more bothersome now than ever before.

"I do not know why I did not tell you I loved you before," he gritted out, "but that does not mean I did not feel the emotion."

Only an idiot would not love this woman.

She took a deep breath and then her expression changed, a seductive light coming into her eyes.

She rose up on her elbow and pushed him backward, her mouth coming within a breath of his. "It's okay, Aristide, really. I don't want to think about before or how you can't remember me now. I just want to make love.

I've missed you and last night didn't begin to make up for it."

No man could stand against such naked provocation. She kissed him and he responded with passion he had thought spent.

Eden lay awake as Aristide slept beside her. They had made love again, this time tenderly and for a very long time. He shouted love words in the midst of his release and she had returned them, but how could she believe his were real?

They had been lovers and then married for a total of three years as of yesterday and not once had a word even slightly resembling love crossed his lips. Tonight was the first time he had ever called her *agape mou* even.

Was it possible that he had truly fallen in love with her? What did that say of the time they had been together before? What if he regained his memory and with it knowledge that what he felt for her was not love?

The questions whirled through her brain, tormenting her thoughts with one unhappy scenario after another.

What if he was only insisting now that he loved her out of guilt? She'd latched on to the fact he wasn't proud of the way he'd treated her up to now, though he seemed too full of macho pride to admit that fact. Could love born of guilt last? Was it even real?

Everything was so confusing. How would she ever know the truth of his feelings when he seemed so intent on proving he was a better husband than her memories indicated?

He was even willing to fire Kassandra. Eden actually thought that might happen now. Aristide in guilt mode (even one he refused to acknowledge) was a fearsome prospect.

She didn't want him coming out of it before Kassandra was gone from their lives, but neither did she want to spend the rest of her life married to a man who stayed with her because he felt badly about the way he'd treated her at first. That was hardly more appetizing a prospect than being married for the sake of their baby.

Aristide walked into his office on Monday morning with an unshakeable sense of purpose.

He had grilled Eden the day before on Kassandra's behavior since the beginning of their marriage and he had no doubts about firing the woman. She had made Eden miserable with her subtle innuendo and manipulations and *he had let her*. That was his cross to bear, but he wasn't letting Kassandra's poison infect his life or torment his wife one more day.

The confrontation went much as he had expected it to after Eden's revelations. Kassandra attempted lies and further manipulations to keep her job and her place in his life, but he refused to be moved.

"You are fired, Kassandra. Security is waiting by your desk with your six months' severance check to walk you out. You no longer have clearance in any of the Kouros Industries buildings or computers."

"You cannot be serious. You can't fire me!"

"You are wrong."

"But you need me, not that American whore. She knows nothing of your business…she cannot even speak our language adequately! I belong by your side, not her!"

"Do not ever call my wife anything like that again… I can ruin you, Kassandra…completely. Do not ever do something that will make me think I have to."

She blanched and then glared, her hands curled at her

sides like claws. "You would have loved me if she had not gotten in the way."

"You were never in the running."

"You made love to me."

"We had sex. Mutually consenting sex without commitment." A brief affair, nothing more. He realized why now. The woman had no heart and he now knew the difference between cold, calculated sex and making love.

Eden made love to him and, God willing, he would never know a time without that gift.

"How dare you? It was not like that. We both enjoyed it." Her anger had twisted her features into an ugly mask. "I am important to you. You need me."

"No, I do not."

The tears spilled over, but for the first time in memory the sight of a woman's distress moved him not one iota.

She stopped at the door and turned back to face him. "She was ready to leave you in New York. She wanted to file for divorce. Did your sainted little wife tell you that?"

Something exploded in his brain, like a wall collapsing into rubble. "You are lying."

"No. You only wish I were. This time I am telling the unvarnished truth. I heard your argument about our trip to the theater. She was so angry, she was spitting mad, but it was nothing like the way she went for you in the car on the way to upstate New York."

"You could not possibly know what was discussed in that car ride."

"Of course I can, I had you bugged." She gave him a pitying look and then affected Eden's American accent. "I can't take it anymore, Aristide. I want a divorce."

With one final glare, Kassandra exited the office, but Aristide barely noticed.

His brain was bombarding him with images. The first time he saw Eden outside the Metropolitan Museum of Art—she had been so beautiful, she entranced him. The first time they made love…the birth of their son…so many pictures flashed through his brain at supersonic speed. Then came the car ride Kassandra mentioned…before the accident.

And he knew exactly what had caused that sense of foreboding that had plagued him since discovering he had a wife he could not remember.

Not for the first time since starting the drive, Aristide wished he'd used his chauffeur-driven car. Eden was intent on having a relationship discussion and he couldn't focus on her and the road at the same time.

"What are you saying?" he asked, sure he must have misunderstood her last words.

"You have a choice to make. It's either your precious assistant or your wife. You can't have both."

He bit back a curse. Eden's hormone-driven irrationality had already spawned one major argument between the two of them; he was determined to avoid another.

She hadn't told him she was pregnant yet, but they shared the same bed and he could count. She hadn't had her menses last month and she'd stopped breast-feeding rather abruptly.

He didn't know why she hadn't told him unless she was saving it as a Christmas surprise, or actually didn't realize it herself yet. She might not have put two and two together as quickly as he had.

He remembered how easily she'd gotten distracted during her pregnancy with Theo. Her scatterbrained mentality had been really endearing, but he had never teased her about it because she had been overly sensitive then too.

"I know you do not mean that."

"And on what evidence do you make that assumption?"

"You love me. You are not going to walk away because you have gotten upset with Kassandra over some trivial thing."

"You consider her attempts to undermine the viability of our marriage trivial?" she asked, her voice colder than he had ever heard it.

Damn it. "I did not say that."

"But you don't believe she's trying to break us up?"

"Listen to yourself, *yineka mou*. Do you not think you are being even a tiny bit dramatic here?"

"No."

He sighed. "Well, you are," he said as gently as he could.

He really did not want to upset her more than she already was.

"I am not being dramatic, but I'm beginning to see you're never going to believe me."

"Be fair. You have never once before this week complained about Kassandra and I have seen with my own eyes her attempts to make you comfortable in a foreign environment."

"Her attempts to show up my ignorance, you mean."

He gritted his teeth, not wanting to lose his temper, but getting angry against his will. "You are not being reasonable."

"What is unreasonable about me wanting my husband to get rid of the woman trying to destroy my marriage?"

"Why would Kassandra want to do that?" he asked, taking another tack. If he could get her to see she was looking at things from a completely illogical point of view, they could end this ludicrous discussion.

"She wants you."

"She is my employee, not my lover."

"She was once, or so she intimated."

Tension gripped him. He had to tread carefully here. He and Kassandra had been lovers once. Very briefly, right around when he met Eden, but once he met his wife, other women stopped existing for him. Kassandra had taken their break-up with the same sophisticated cool she responded to everything else. Neither her heart nor her pride had been particularly affected.

"No way would she say that to you."

"You are wrong."

"Eden…" he growled, his growing frustration making his voice harsh.

"Oh, I forgot, you don't believe anything I say about your precious employee."

"Stop calling her that. The only woman around here who is precious to me is you, even when you are being irrationally jealous," he said teasingly, trying to defuse the tension growing between them.

"I am not irrational and I accepted a long time ago I am not precious to you either."

"What the hell do you mean by that?" he asked in a near roar, losing his hold on his temper.

"Just what I said. I knew you didn't love me when we got married, but I thought my love would make it all right. I was wrong. I've found that being married for the sake of my child and tolerated for the sake of my talent in bed isn't enough. It hurts too much."

"This has gone far enough. You are completely without reason and perhaps your condition is at fault, but you will stop making these wild accusations immediately."

"You're not in the boardroom, Aristide. You cannot

order me around like one of your directors." Then she went silent and stayed that way for several seconds.

Good. Maybe she was calming down.

"You know I am pregnant." She said it in a flat voice, void of the joy such an announcement should bring.

"I am sorry if I stole your thunder, but, yes, I know."

"Since when?"

"Since you missed your first period and started craving burnt toast for breakfast in the morning."

"So, when you invited me to come with you to New York, you knew?" Why did she sound so passionless, as if her emotions were in lock-down mode?

"Yes, I knew."

"That explains it. I had hoped… It doesn't matter. I was wrong."

"What did you hope?"

"That you had finally gotten tired of being apart from me, that you wanted our marriage to be a closer one. Isn't that a joke?" she asked with bitter cynicism he hadn't thought her capable of.

"I do not like being apart from you."

Once he realized she was pregnant again, he also realized he was tired of leaving her behind in Greece when he traveled. He had ordered one of the jets to be equipped for travel with infants so she could come with him, but he hadn't told her.

He had wanted to save it as a Christmas surprise…a sort of reciprocal gift for her new pregnancy.

She laughed, the sound strained and blackly amused. "Right. How could you possibly miss me when you've got super-Kassandra along for the ride?"

"She is not my wife."

"She would like to be."

"That is nonsense."

Eden didn't reply to that. In fact, she said nothing for several miles.

It started to rain and he turned on the wipers. "We should be there soon." As conversation gambits went it was not great, but he was leery of starting yet another volatile argument.

"I think it would be best if we separated," she said in a weary, dead voice. "I can move back to New York, or move into a separate residence near Athens if you still feel strongly about the children being raised in Greece. We can work out visitation either way."

He felt like someone had punched him straight in the chest and the air seized in his lungs. He turned to look at her, needing to know if she was serious, hoping with everything in him she was not.

Her eyes were filled with pain-filled determination. "I can't take it anymore, Aristide. I want a divorce."

He couldn't breathe. His chest hurt. She had gone from, "I think we need to separate," to "I want a divorce," in a heartbeat.

He started yelling at her, but it took several seconds of no response and a sideways glance that revealed her blank-eyed regard for him to realize he'd been doing so in Greek. He shouted the one English word he could get out, "No!"

But it was lost in her scream and his eyes snapped back to the road to see a truck had swerved into their lane.

He had no time to maneuver. She would be hurt. He could lose her. He flung his arm out to protect her even as he tried to avoid the unavoidable.

He woke up. Lying beside the road. His head hurt and he could make little sense of the sounds swirling around him.

"Doesn't look good…blood…nothing we can do…unlikely…survive…" He slipped back into unconsciousness, certain his wife and unborn baby were going to die.

Aristide sat at his desk, shaking and sweating.

His wife had survived the crash, but had his baby? He remembered she had not been at his bedside during his coma… Kassandra had convinced him it meant Eden did not really care about him. But she had been hospitalized herself…not merely for a minor concussion…but for a miscarriage as well?

He picked up the phone and asked to be put through to the hospital in New York in a voice weak from the horror of his memories. Some time later, he put the phone down again, relief coursing through him. She had not lost the baby, but once again she had not told him about it either. Why not?

Then he laughed derisively at himself and his obtuseness.

She'd told him he married her solely for the sake of their unborn son and she had believed it. She had kept the baby out of the equation this time because she wanted to be the deciding factor in the way he felt about their marriage now. Or did she?

According to the memories torturing his mind, his wife wanted a divorce.

Bile rose in his throat. He had never told her he loved her and she believed he didn't. She had spent their entire time together believing she was nothing special to him when she was the very air he breathed.

He had not said the words, but, damn it, how could she not have known? He needed her in a way he had never and could never need another human being.

She hadn't left him after the hospital. In fact, she had

acted like she wanted to salvage their marriage. Did she, or was that an act born of her tenderhearted nature? Was she holding off leaving him because of his amnesia? If he told her he could remember, would she walk out?

She certainly hadn't believed him when he told her he loved her last night, so in her mind, nothing was changed between them. She still didn't trust him and why should she? He'd done little enough to earn that trust. But he had fired Kassandra.

That had to be good for something.

None of it mattered if he couldn't convince her that he loved her, though. His mind spun with possibilities and he thought he came up with just the way to do it, but first he had to finish the courtship he'd started the day before.

He picked up the phone again; this time, he called a florist.

Eden felt like laughing out loud as yet another delivery arrived.

The first had been a huge bouquet of scarlet roses. The card attached had read, "You have my passion forever."

Then every hour on the hour, a new delivery arrived, each of them an arrangement of six yellow roses in a crystal vase. The card with these all read the same thing: "Yellow roses are for everlasting love…these are tokens of mine."

He really wanted her to believe he loved her. She was beginning to think that, regardless of what he had felt for her for three years, he really did love her now…maybe even as much as she loved him.

At four o'clock, there was no ringing of the doorbell with another delivery, but at four-fifteen, Aristide walked into the living room.

She was playing with the baby like she did every afternoon, this time facing the hall. She had been waiting for him and only now realized it. Her hungry gaze took in his features with joy.

He was dressed in one of his custom-tailored business suits and carried a crystal vase filled with six yellow roses just like the others.

She surged to her feet like a puppet on strings, controlled by his presence.

He smiled at her. "*Agape mou*, you look beautiful."

She laughed. She couldn't help it. She was wearing a T-shirt and jeans like she usually did when playing with their rambunctious son. Not exactly beauty queen material.

Aristide presented her with the flowers.

She took them and immediately buried her face in the fragrant blooms. "They're wonderful."

"Yellow roses are for everlasting love."

She lifted her head. "So the cards all said."

"Each one represents a month I have felt that way about you."

Including this vase, that would make thirty-six…the total number of months since they met. "That's impossible. I told you—"

His finger pressed against her lips. "I know what you believed, but you were wrong, my precious Eden, so very wrong."

She stared at him…had he remembered? But, no, he would have said. "How can you be so sure?"

"Because I know myself and I know that I could not love you this much now and not have loved you at all before. That is quite impossible."

Could it be true? Had she misjudged her husband's feelings for her? Like she had told Aristide, he had never once told her he *didn't* love her, he had just never told her that he did.

She turned and put the flowers on a nearby table then turned back and threw herself in her husband's arms. "It doesn't matter, if you love me now. It doesn't matter."

But it did. Aristide wanted to tell his wife he remembered, but he didn't want to risk her walking away before he got a chance to convince her of his love. She needed to believe without a doubt that his love for her was genuine. He hoped the plans he had set in motion today would be sufficient evidence.

They were in bed that night when he told her about firing Kassandra.

"She said you were on the verge of divorcing me," he said, fishing for her feelings on the matter now.

Eden paled, but she nodded. "It's true."

"Do you still feel that way?" he asked.

She looked down at their entwined naked bodies pointedly. "What do you think?"

"I think you are very generous, but why did you stay with me?"

"The doctor said not to upset you, that it could be very risky to a concussed patient. I thought telling you that the wife you could not remember wanted a divorce fell under the label of upsetting news."

He hadn't considered that angle, but it supported his worry that she stayed out of concern for him, not desire.

"I love you."

A shadow passed through her gaze, but she nodded and then kissed him long and hard. She still wasn't sure of him, but she would be.

Eventually, she settled back against his arm. "How did Kassandra know about me asking for a divorce?"

"She placed a pen with a listening device in the rental car."

"That's deranged!"

"Or determined. I put security on it immediately. They discovered that she had purchased two such devices over the Internet a month before our trip to New York. The other one was found in her apartment when it was searched."

"She let you search?"

"She was facing major charges being filed if she did not."

"She wanted to marry you."

"Yes, but she did not understand that love cannot be replaced by sex and ambition. She does not and never did love me, but she wanted more power than she had as my personal assistant. She thought she deserved it because of our lifelong friendship."

"I still say that makes her sick."

"Probably. It also makes her virtually unemployable."

"You're not keeping it quiet? What if the press picks up the story?"

"She should have considered the possibilities before playing her ruthless games with my life."

"Greeks really do have a thing with revenge, don't they?"

"My father used to say that bad behavior is its own revenge. He was right. Everything happening to Kassandra right now, she brought on herself through her actions."

"I'm glad she's out of our lives."

"I am too."

She was silent so long it made him nervous. "What?"

"I just can't believe everything is so different now."

"Wait until Christmas and you will find out how different."

She sat bolt upright and demanded, "What kind of different?"

"You will have to wait and see."

She immediately started badgering him for answers and he laughed, reveling in his ability to remember this endearing trait. She couldn't stand knowing she had a surprise waiting for her…she wanted to know everything right now.

She had wanted to know the sex of their child before Theo's birth and had spent hours researching genetics trying to figure out what color of eyes and hair he would have.

In the end, the only way to stop her questions was to make love to her and it was no hardship.

CHAPTER TWELVE

THEY WENT to the island for Christmas. No one minded the change in plans, but Eden wanted to know if it had something to do with her surprise. Aristide refused to enlighten her.

Sebastian, Rachel and the children joined them, as did Phillippa and Vincent.

Eden was awed by how beautifully the small island church had been decorated for the holiday and thought they should make coming to the island for Christmas a tradition. Red, white and pink poinsettias were everywhere, along with yards and yards of green garland and holly. Gold silk draped the pews with green-and-red velvet ribbon accents.

She could not wait for the candlelight service on Christmas Eve.

Music outside her window woke Eden on Christmas Eve morning. It didn't sound like Christmas carols, but she wasn't familiar with all the Greek forms of the festive music. She reached for Aristide's warmth without opening her eyes and frowned when her questing hand found only an empty bed.

Her eyes slid open and she saw that their room was empty. The *en suite* door was open and the light off. So, he wasn't in there. She threw the covers back to get up and go looking for her errant husband when the door burst open.

Phillippa and Rachel came in, both of their arms overflowing with garment bags and shoeboxes. There was lots and lots of white and Rachel carried a bouquet of white poinsettias, Christmas greenery and gold ribbon in one of her hands.

A strange sensation came over Eden. She remembered her sister-in-law telling her about Sebastian's attempt at a surprise wedding and her throat constricted. Was the pile of white silk in Phillippa's arms what she thought it was?

"*Kalimera*, Eden." Phillippa grinned. "And happy Christmas."

"Good morning to you—what's going on?" she asked in a breathless voice she barely recognized.

"Aristide has arranged a small surprise for you."

"The small surprise comes with a wedding dress?"

Rachel nodded, her own lovely face creased in a happy smile.

Tears filled Eden's eyes. "Oh…I…"

"I trust you are going to take this news better than my other daughter by marriage took the news of her own upcoming wedding."

Rachel blushed, looking chagrined. "I screamed."

Eden shook her head, her throat tight, but she forced out words. "I won't scream. I'm overwhelmed."

"Good." Phillippa took over then.

Within two hours Eden had eaten a small, but wonderful breakfast and was dressed as beautifully as any bride in history. Her gown fit her to perfection, not only in size but in design.

She stood before the mirror. "I look like a fairy princess."

And she did. The dress shimmered with gems and the kerchief-style skirt floated around her legs and ankles in several layers of iridescent silk. The bodice emphasized her small breasts without making them look meager and the jewelencrusted ribbons woven through her hair gave her a definitely ethereal appearance.

There was a knock at the door and butterflies filled her insides.

Phillippa grinned and Rachel opened the door.

Aristide stood on the other side, Sebastian beside him carrying Theo, his own two small children standing beside them.

She had eyes only for her husband. He was dressed in a white tuxedo with long tails and looked so happy she thought her own heart would burst.

He dropped to one knee and took her trembling hand in his own. "Eden Kouros, I have loved you from the first moment and I will love you into eternity. Will you do me the honor of promising yourself to me before my family?"

Before she could reply, his voice gruff, he said, "I really have loved you since the first."

"But…" Her voice trailed off as she noticed something different about his eyes.

It had been there for the past week, but she had thought it was just his newfound love for her.

"You remember," she choked out.

"Yes."

He had a lot of explaining to do…later.

"I would be honored to promise myself to you, Aristide. I love you so much."

His face shone with relief and it was only then that she realized he had been unsure of her answer, and he had asked her in such a public manner anyway.

He stood and put his hand out. She took it and he led her on the traditional walk to the church. Dozens of people joined along the way and she realized from the familiar faces that many of the Kouros and Demakis clans had come to the island for the festivities.

They stopped outside the church to observe the ritual of drinking from the same cup and then proceeded inside.

The tiara he placed on her head glittered with diamonds and her favorite mystic topaz, his simpler crown looked old and she remembered seeing it in his parents' wedding pictures. It was the one his father had worn to marry his mother. For some reason that struck her as even more wonderful than everything else and she smiled lovingly at him through a mist of tears she didn't even try to blink away.

The ceremony was beautiful and, as he had once told her, there was no vow of fidelity, but the promise was in his eyes and her heart reacted to it with joyous acceptance.

The reception was big and boisterous with dancing and a lot of celebrating, ending with the candlelight Christmas Eve service.

It was much later when the other guests had left that she and Aristide were allowed to go to their room in privacy. Theo had long since gone to bed.

"When did you remember?" she asked after he carried her inside and lowered himself into a chair, seating her in his lap.

"The morning I fired Kassandra."

The day he had sent her all the roses, saying he had always loved her. "Why didn't you say something then?"

"I wanted to be sure you knew I loved you first."

"But why?"

"You told me you wanted a divorce. How could I be sure you wouldn't ask for one again once you figured out I remembered?"

"That's stupid! Why would I want a divorce now?"

"I did not know why you wanted a divorce then," he reminded her in a voice that reflected the pain of the conversation in the car on that fateful day.

"Do you understand now?" she asked.

"Yes, but, damn it, how could you be so mistaken about me not loving you?"

She couldn't believe he had to ask. *"You never told me any differently."*

"That was an unquestionably imprudent oversight, but I loved you with my body every time we joined as you loved me with yours. I was besotted and I find it difficult to believe you could not see that. I lost sleep, skipped meetings and turned my schedule upside down to visit you in upstate New York as often as I could when we were lovers."

"I didn't know our time together was such a tremendous hardship on your schedule."

"I am the President of Oversees Operations for a huge company…do you really think I routinely had weekends free during those months?"

"I didn't take that into account…" But that wasn't true.

She *had* considered it at first and taken it as evidence she was someone special to him, but even knowing what she did about her father's schedule, she hadn't begun to realize what the time with her had cost Aristide.

And later, when she had begun to truly doubt his feelings for her, she had dismissed the importance of that time entirely. She had seen only that none of that time included the other people closest to him in his life.

"I married you, Eden…did you think that meant nothing?"

"You married me for Theo's sake."

"When did I ever say that?"

"You didn't ask me until I told you I was pregnant."

"But if I had not loved you, I would not have asked you then. Perhaps I did not call the emotion by its proper name at the time…even to myself, but it was there. Be assured of it. After the example of my uncle's marriage, I would never have risked marriage for anything less." He smiled, the expression going straight to her heart. "And before you start creating any more wild scenarios, I did not organize this wedding because of the new baby either."

"You know…?"

"I remembered everything. I had some pretty terrifying moments waiting for word from the hospital in New York however." He put his hand protectively over her womb. "I am very happy you are pregnant again."

"No concerns about a lack of proper spacing between our children?" she teased.

He looked blank for a second and then his gaze sharpened with understanding and his hand pressed possessively against her. "None whatsoever."

She was glad he knew about the baby and relieved he had thought to contact the hospital instead of worrying they had lost their child. She was even happier he was thrilled about the news, but had she really ever doubted that response?

"I concede you did not marry me this time for the child," she said with a smile.

"And that I loved you all along?"

"If you loved me, why did you leave me in Greece while you traveled so much?"

Dull color scored his cheeks. "I would like to say I had no choice and, in some instances, that was true. I really did worry about you traveling during your pregnancy…you were so sick at first. Then, later, I did not know how easily a baby would travel. Sebastian has been content to allow me to do most of the traveling for Kouros Industries since before his marriage to Rachel."

"You said you would like to say that was the reason…" She already knew it wasn't entirely valid, not for all the trips, and he was smart enough to realize it.

"The truth is all those trips were me being stupid again. You were right, I was not entirely ready for the commitment of marriage, but not for the reasons you thought. I had committed to you in those ways from the first time we made love, but you have more power over me than anyone ever has."

"And you are used to absolute control."

"Yes."

"How was being apart supposed to make that better?"

"I thought I could keep a lid on it if I did not get too dependent on you. This thinking began when we were lovers and continued after our marriage, but every trip I took was harder to go on. Every time I left I wanted to come home more. Surely you noticed how short my trips had become."

"I was too busy being miserably certain you didn't love me and never would."

"I called you all the time…do you think I did that with any other woman? I do not even call my mother as often."

She laughed at that. "I didn't consider multiple phone calls evidence of life-long loving devotion."

"You should have."

She almost laughed, but he seemed so serious. "Maybe I should have, but you didn't introduce me to your family the whole time we were lovers."

This time the red in his cheeks was dark and anything but subtle. "I knew if my mother or brother knew of you, they would disapprove."

"They would think I wasn't good enough for you? Because I wasn't Greek?"

"Because it would be obvious to anyone after ten minutes in our company that I had seduced you into anticipating our wedding vows. My mother would have been ashamed of me. You should have seen her with Sebastian over Rachel. It was not pretty. At first I was not ready to get married and then I was too content keeping you all to myself. I knew as soon as I married you, I would have to share you with everyone...not just my family. And I knew if I shared you with my family, we would end up married very quickly."

"That's—"

"Heinously selfish, I know."

"Sweet, I was about to say."

He seemed to relax a little. "I am glad you see it that way." He took a deep breath. "I talked with Dr Lewis for over an hour when I called the hospital. I know why I forgot you."

Scared—even though her heart and the way he held her told her she shouldn't be—she asked, "Why?"

"I woke beside the road, after the accident. I was really out of it, but I overheard the paramedics saying something about not being able to do anything for you...I thought you were going to die."

"They were talking about the baby."

"That is what Dr Lewis said."

"How could Adam know? He wasn't there."

"He surmised from their report."

"Oh…"

"I do not like you calling him Adam."

She stifled a grin. "American doctors are not as formal as Greek doctors."

"So I noticed."

"So you forgot me because you thought I was going to die?"

"Doctor Lewis thinks that on top of the trauma of you asking for a divorce, that belief triggered my mind into forgetting in self-protection."

"You told the doctor what I said in the car?"

"Yes. I had to know why I would forget you and he insisted on knowing everything before helping me figure it out."

"Wow. You really did love me."

His eyes filled with deep, dark emotion. "I could not face life without you…I still cannot."

"You should have said."

"I will spend the rest of my life saying it a hundred times a day."

"At least."

They both smiled, the love between them so tangible she had to ask herself how she could have been so sure it did not exist before. But she knew.

"Remember, I told you my dad had had affairs."

"Yes. He is not the most devoted of fathers either. Business always comes first."

"I thought it did with you too, but I see now how I was coloring you with his behavior."

"I made mistakes, but you and our family mean more to me than anything, *yineka mou*."

"I'm glad. You mean more than anything to me too." She snuggled into Aristide's lap. "My dad said he loved my mom and then had multiple affairs. She died of cancer when I was thirteen. He nursed her so carefully, so lovingly through it all, but all I could remember were the nights I could hear her crying when he was out with one of his women."

"You did not trust men."

"No."

"I am not your father."

"No, quite the opposite. You have been as faithful as a man can be, but did not tell me you loved me. I should have been okay with that, you know?"

"My refusal to say the words made you insecure. Kassandra's innuendos did not help."

She leaned back to look directly into his eyes, her own wet with happy moisture. "I'm sorry I ever accused you of having an affair."

"I am sorry for so much I cannot begin to say it all, but it will be different from now on."

"Yes, we'll both be smarter."

"We will love each other forever." He kissed her and they sealed their very personal vows in a very personal way.

They opened gifts Christmas Day, the children going first and then playing with their new toys on the floor amidst a pile of colorful paper while the adults opened theirs.

Phillippa and Vincent loved their trip of the most famous gardens of the world that the men and their wives had arranged.

"Eden did most of the arranging, I'm sure you won't be surprised to hear," Rachel said laughingly.

Phillippa's look of loving joy made Eden blush and duck her head before anyone saw the tears in her eyes. Pregnancy hormones were the pits sometimes.

When she opened her gift from Aristide, she didn't understand what she was looking at. "You bought me a plane?"

He shook his head and laughed. "I had one of the Kouros jets outfitted for family travel."

She looked more closely at the pictures in the flat gold box and sucked in a breath of joy. "You really aren't planning to leave me behind anymore, are you?"

"No. We will have to stop traveling the last month of your pregnancy, but other than that, nothing will hold us back."

The room erupted with news of the baby and it was a long time before she and Aristide had a moment alone with their son. They were tucking him into his crib for his nap and Aristide had his arms around Eden while she soothed their son to sleep.

"We are a family, *agape mou*."

"A loving family," she affirmed.

They quietly crept from the baby's room. He suggested taking a walk down to the small church and she gladly went, loving this new open rapport they shared…the security she felt in his feelings for her.

They stopped in front of the altar where many candles burned.

He turned to face her, his eyes suspiciously bright. "The first Christmas after we met, I came here and thanked God for the gift of the woman who would become my wife."

She opened her mouth, but nothing would come out.

He kissed her softly.

"That was only a few days after we met."

"Yes."

"You knew then that you wanted to marry me?"

"I knew then that I *would* marry you, that you would be the mother of my children. I made mistakes, but never doubt that you have had my love all along."

"I won't. I won't ever doubt you again, my love."

He took her into his arms and pressed his lips to hers, the smell of Christmas greenery surrounding them in the small church that had hosted their marriage born of true love.

If you enjoyed what you just read,
then we've got an offer you can't resist!

Take 2 bestselling
love stories FREE!
Plus get a FREE surprise gift!